39 DAYS

Based on a True Story of Brutal Murder, Calculated Revenge, and Questionable Justice

M ICHAEL W HAN

authorHOUSE®

AuthorHouse™
1663 Liberty Drive
Bloomington, IN 47403
www.authorhouse.com
Phone: 1-800-839-8640

First published by AuthorHouse   8/31/2009

ISBN: 978-1-4490-1651-7 (e)
ISBN: 978-1-4490-1649-4 (sc)
ISBN: 978-1-4490-1650-0 (hc)

Printed in the United States of America
Bloomington, Indiana

This book is printed on acid-free paper.

39 DAYS

Based on a true story of brutal murder, calculated revenge, and questionable justice

PROLOGUE

DAY 36

<u>Friday, 10:45 AM — Pico Rivera, California</u>

Officer Dennis Patrick wasn't used to being so far out of his territory. For the past seven years, D-Pat (as he was known to his coworkers and friends) had been assigned to a twelve-mile radius in Pico Rivera, California. At one time, Pico Rivera had been considered a suburb of Los Angeles, but now that all these smaller cities had been swallowed up by the ever-expanding boundaries of Los Angeles, it was no different from any other LA district. In the case of Pico, it was 80 percent Hispanic, relatively poor (meaning most inhabitants had jobs that paid by the hour), and extremely tough.

Dennis would rarely let down his guard while on patrol in Pico, because the anti-police sentiment among certain Pico residents was high, and self-restraint was low. He had learned early on to pick his battles wisely in this area. If he wanted to, he could simply sit at specific street corners, parking lots, or alleys and wait for a drug transaction or domestic disturbance to come to him, but arresting fifteen-year-olds all day did very little to keep Pico safe.

Dennis proudly boasted that despite seven years on the job in Pico Rivera, he had only pulled his gun from its holster two times, and had only been forced to physically overpower a suspect once.

He'd witnessed things he'd never forget and forgotten things most people would never witness. He was proud of his record in Pico, and was even prouder of the relationships he had formed with some of the neighborhood's long-standing residents. Despite the poverty, racial tensions, and influence of gang-related activity, Dennis remained convinced that the overwhelming majority of Pico residents were good people, and they respected the job he did.

Like any city, or any assignment he might receive, he spent 90 percent of his time with the 10 percent of people who don't respect police, don't respect others, and aren't afraid to physically force their ideas on those who stand in their way.

Today, however, was the first time he'd been asked to leave his territory during an official shift. Sure, he had to be downtown LA to appear in court every few days or so, to represent the state on tickets or fines he had written -- or to occasionally testify as to certain evidence or conversations that he had been privy to -- but today was much different.

"D-Pat, the captain wants to see you, pronto," his shift leader, Sergeant John Nelson, had said as Dennis entered the locker-room facility at the Pico Rivera Police Department.

"You sure you got the right guy?" Dennis asked, wondering why the heck Captain Sturgess would need to see him.

"Probably needs a ride to the airport or someone to check to see if his wife is cheating on him again," Sergeant Nelson joked, as he could see that Dennis was a bit rattled by the request.

"Shit, if he needed to know if his wife was cheating, that's easy," said Dennis, "I'll just tell him I've seen your car at his house every afternoon this week, Sarg."

Dennis chuckled and gave the sergeant a joking forearm to the chest as he exited the locker room.

"D-Pat, I got no time to do the captain's wife," Sergeant Nelson yelled back as Dennis was leaving, "since your girlfriend has got me completely worn out."

Dennis kept walking. He enjoyed a good locker-room ribbing as much as the next guy, but in seven years on this assignment, this was the first time Captain Sturgess had ever requested a one-on-one meeting with Dennis, and he certainly wasn't going to keep him waiting.

As he approached the captain's corner office, his heart started pounding so hard that he was actually afraid it might be noticeable through his uniform. Now he wished he had armored up --meaning put on his flak jacket -- prior to coming to see the captain, as the jacket would have eliminated any noticeable heartbeats and probably made him look a little more official.

The captain's door was always closed -- always. Dennis guessed Captain Sturgess hadn't seen the training video regarding the open-door policy of the LAPD.

Dennis tapped lightly on the door and waited for a response.

"D-Pat, is that you?" the captain yelled.

"Yes, captain."

"Get in here," Captain Sturgess said in the friendliest tone he could muster.

DAY 36

The Riverside County Medical Examiner turned into the warehouse office complex and carefully navigated her van between six or seven police squad cars randomly located in the parking lot.

The call to her office had said probable murder, so she had appropriately braced herself for what she might encounter. Now, in her fifth year on the job, Natalie Fulson wasn't rattled by much. Gang shootings, automobile collisions, and teenage drug overdoses used to freeze her in her tracks; but five years later, she had hardened her senses and was now able to categorize every crime or accident scene as "just her job."

"Morning, Nat," Officer Tom Kiley, or TK to his close friends, was the first to greet her. TK was always friendly, but today he seemed especially cordial. When he saw her get out of her van, she noticed that he quickly crossed the parking lot to meet her.

"Whadda we got, TK?" Nat said, assuming Tom had been at the scene for quite a while.

"We got something," TK said with noticeable caution and apprehension in his voice, "that is beyond description."

"Nat," he said as he looked back over his shoulder toward the loading dock door that opened to one of the warehouses, "this is some nasty stuff."

Natalie had long ago learned not to question patrol cops about the details of the crime scene, as they almost always included their own thoughts and biases about what happened. So despite TK's open-ended

7

comment about what was in the warehouse, she decided to remain quiet and simply go see for herself.

"Anybody pick up for this one?" Natalie asked. If there was one thing that Nat could count on, it was coffee at a crime scene. Usually the first cop on the scene would rope it off and call it in. The second cop was usually responsible for taking quotes from witnesses or interviewing people in the immediate area. The third cop was the key to a good crime scene, because as patrolmen liked to say, "three means tea." Probably a carryover saying that dates back to Britain, where tea was an all-day drink, but regardless of where the saying originated, it was certainly still a habit for Nat's local police force.

"Trust me on this one, Nat," said TK, "this one is better off on an empty stomach."

TK's comments caught Nat a bit off guard. She'd known Officer Tom Kiley for almost four years, and in all that time she couldn't think of another crime scene, or accident scene, that had noticeably bothered him. Maybe he had been affected by previous cases, but he surely never let her, or anyone else, know it.

"Okay, caffeine can wait. Take me to your stiff," Nat joked.

Even as she said it aloud, she was disappointed with herself. When Nat first joined the coroner's office, it used to drive her nuts that the detectives, cops, and paramedics were so casual about victims. Terms like *stiffs, floaters, beanbags,* and *piñatas* used to make her cringe. A deceased human being was still someone's dad, mom, brother, cousin, or friend. It took her a long time to get used to the lingo of the crime scene, but she always secretly vowed not to become "one of them."

Now she was using a term like stiff before she even got out of the parking lot. She silently scolded herself as she followed TK across the lot.

"This warehouse has been empty for about a year," TK explained as they walked toward a raised loading dock, typically used for loading and unloading semi-trailers. "It used to be an office supply outfit that would cater to small businesses in the area. You know, paper, ink cartridges, envelopes, that sort of stuff."

"Why'd they move out? It seems like that kind of stuff would thrive in a business park area like this?" Nat questioned. She was always a little fascinated by how building tenants seemed to be constantly turning over.

"Office Depot moved in about eighteen months ago and essentially terminated all these small local operations," TK said as he pointed in the general direction of the Office Depot Superstore that everyone knew about -- and Natalie was no exception. "Big bastards move in, and the little guy either joins up, if he can," TK paused as if just saying it aloud was bothering him even more, "or finds a new career."

"You sound pissed, TK. You a secret investor in an office supplies operation or something like that?" Nat chuckled.

"No, no, no," TK said as if her question had actually been serious. "I have a neighbor that was in the hardware business, and his forced early retirement was courtesy of the Home Depot." TK stared at Nat, waiting for some kind of response, and when he didn't get one, he added, "I guess it just touches a nerve with me."

Natalie followed TK up the four or five stairs that led to the dock platform, and from there they entered through the fire escape door, which had been opened for them.

It was immediately obvious that the warehouse was empty, other than rows and rows of metal racking. Natalie was struck with how quickly all daylight seems to vanish when you step inside a huge concrete box, with no windows, thirty-foot-high ceilings, and only one open bay door.

"Please tell me electricity is still turned on," Nat pleaded, "as my normal shoddy work gets even worse when it's done in the dark."

One of the other patrolmen who stood by the open bay door chimed in. "Yes ma'am, but the lights in here are on candescent bulbs, so they take about ten minutes to kick in."

"Please, save the term *ma'am* for someone much older and much higher in rank," Natalie corrected. "When did you throw the switch?" Nat asked, so she could work backward against his ten-minute estimate.

"They should pop on any minute," said the young, baby-faced officer, who seemed somewhat embarrassed by his ma'am comment.

As Natalie and TK stepped farther into the warehouse, she could see that the metal racking reached all the way from the floor, to just three or four feet from the ceiling. The racks were painted orange and were bolted to the floor.

"All the way back here," TK said, giving her a half-hearted wave toward the third aisle of racking.

The farther they got, the less Natalie could see, so she tried to time her walk to keep perfect pace with TK. She listened to his boots against the concrete floor and tried to match each stride -- that way she wouldn't lose him or run into him.

Just as she was completely focused on her steps, the overhead lights of the jumbo-sized warehouse sprang to life. In an instant, the sixty-thousand-square-foot warehouse, perhaps the size of a football field, was completely visible.

Natalie's first view was of TK. He was looking almost straight up, and the look on his face was terrifying. Sometimes in her business, watching the reaction of someone else could actually be worse than looking directly at the victim. Unfortunately, as she followed his gaze to the scene above them, Natalie realized that TK's reaction was the absolute least of her problems.

While the dizziness she immediately felt told her brain to look away, she was unable to break her gaze on this unbelievable sight.

DAYS 1 – 8

NEVER MET ... NEVER FORGOTTEN

DAY 1

Friday, 10:50 PM -- "A Taste of LA" City Fair, Los Angeles, California

Juan Alvarez stood by the ticket window at the local street fair and scanned the crowd. He had told his younger brother to meet him at this exact location at 10:30 pm. He wasn't surprised that Hector was a no-show. Hector was nineteen years old on the outside, but still thirteen or fourteen on the inside. If he found a better invitation for tonight's festivities, he wouldn't think twice about bailing on his older brother. Hector owned a cell phone, but he rarely ever answered it, as he always thought life was more important than any text message or phone call.

Juan nervously made one last pass through the crowd, but he was certain that Hector wasn't there. Juan silently prayed that his younger sibling wasn't doing something stupid, as Hector had a unique way of filling his free time with law-breaking activities. Juan hadn't noticed the band of girls watching him from the other side of the street. Typical of Juan, he always focused on Hector and his family responsibilities before any personal fun. As he glanced at his watch, he finally gave up on Hector and started back toward his car.

The girls giggled, as they secretly captured pictures of Juan on their tiny cell phones. Juan was not only an attractive, strong twenty-two-year old, but he also moved like an elite athlete -- confident, assured, and graceful. The girls joked about which one of them should approach the sexy stranger, but like always, it was Angelina who simply stepped away from the pack and started walking toward Juan at a pace that left the others behind.

Juan's car was parked on the street just a block and a half from the City Fair, and as he got close to the vehicle, he unlocked the doors with his remote key. As he slid into the driver's seat, Angelina surprised him by quickly jumping in the passenger side.

"Where we goin'?" Angelina giggled as she attached her seat belt.

"What the hell?" Juan said nervously as his eyes darted around to see if there was anyone else with her. When he calmed himself in realizing that she was alone, he continued, "Who the hell are you?"

"I'm your date," Angelina said with her best, most seductive smile. After a slight pause, she questioned, "That is, if you're up for a little fun?"

Juan, who wasn't really known for his spontaneous actions, had to pause for a second to collect his thoughts. This unknown passenger was certainly beautiful; there was no question about that. Hector seemed like he'd made his own plans for the night, and as a result, Juan really didn't have anywhere he needed to be.

So without another word, Juan started the car and headed out for what his mystery date had classified as "a little fun."

DAY 4

Monday, 8:04 am -- Superior Court of Los Angeles County, California

At just after 8 am, Judge Michael Henderson stepped into his office, or his chambers as it was known to lawyers and his clerks. His legs were stiff from yesterday's pickup basketball games. At forty-nine years of age and with fifteen extra pounds on his six-foot, four-inch frame, his joints sounded more like rusty folding chairs, but the judge just couldn't give up his favorite lunchtime activity.

For twelve years, Judge Henderson had always followed the exact same morning routine:

- remove his suit jacket and hang it in the closet
- check his phone messages that had been neatly aligned on his desk, via three-by-five-inch slips of pink paper
- retrieve his handheld tape recorder from his upper-right-hand drawer and insert a new tape
- grab the top case folder from the stack located on the left side of his desk and begin reading (occasionally stopping to dictate notes or responses)

His wife, his clerks, and certainly his children had all made their best attempt to get him "into the twenty-first century," but Judge Henderson was a creature of habit, and he had no intention of ever exchanging his trusty Dictaphone machine for a laptop computer.

First up today was case number RL8348, State of California v. José Seneca Ramirez. The judge couldn't help but cringe as he read the title of the file.

"José, how did you get back so soon?" the judge muttered to himself.

Like many of Judge Henderson's cases, José a was a "regular" -- twenty-three years old; from San Gabriel, California; known gang member; six prior arrests; two prior jail terms; seven-year sentence for breaking and entering (two years served); three-year sentence for domestic battery (one year served).

Clicking the record button on his handheld device, Judge Henderson began dictating notes.

"Helen, please pull the full file on José Seneca Ramirez, of San Gabriel, California," he said slowly, spelling the last name, letter by letter, so that Helen wouldn't have to guess. "When did we last sentence him? How long did he serve against that sentence? Also, please pull the parole board's memo from his latest release."

He put his head back on his oversized leather chair and took a deep breath. There were many things about this job that were truly outstanding, but every time he saw a name like José Ramirez, he questioned whether he was simply wasting his time as a superior court judge of Los Angeles County.

He knew what this brief would say even before he started to read. In fact, he'd read José's story at least three times in the past six or seven years. Like most of his regulars, José was not affected by jail time or state-run rehabilitation programs. José was 100 percent criminal, and the end of his story was 100 percent predictable. The judge knew that José's final destination was a given -- sooner or later José would end up in jail for life or dead in the streets. In that, there was no question. The only question regarding a regular like José Ramirez, and hundreds of others just like him, was how much pain and havoc they would cause between now and their final destination.

Judge Henderson opened his eyes, grabbed the file, and began reading the predictable conclusions. He wished he had the power to prevent José's wrath on mankind, but until José committed a crime that would mandate a life sentence without parole, the judge was only biding time.

DAY 5
Tuesday, 1:05 pm -- St. Mary's Church of Hope, Pico Rivera, California

Hector Alvarez's nineteen-year-old body had never been so filled with emotion as he watched his cousins carry his brother's casket down the church stairs to the waiting hearse. In thirty minutes, the same group would load the casket onto the machine that would lower his brother's twenty-two-year-old, lifeless body into the grave. His brother would be buried two plots over from his mother, who had died giving birth to Hector, and immediately next to his father, who had died ten years earlier in a fight in prison, where he had been serving seven years for an assault-and-battery conviction.

Hector's body literally shook, as if he was chilled to the bone and couldn't get warm. However, the shaking was far deeper than anything caused by temperature change or illness. Hector's reaction was a combination of pain, frustration, and extreme anger.

The pain came from the fact that he was the last Alvarez, at least in his immediate family, left on this planet. After his father's death, his older brother, Juan, had been the clear leader in his life. Juan was in charge of Hector, and he had taken that position very seriously. He made sure that Hector had whatever he needed -- money, trustworthy friends, opportunity, and the right "help" whenever Hector got himself in trouble (which, unfortunately, had been fairly often). Hector had long ago realized that Juan had sacrificed his own life in order to ensure that Hector was safe and happy. Now it occurred to Hector that Juan had quite literally sacrificed his life, and as a result, Hector had never felt so much loneliness and so much pain at the same time.

The frustration Hector felt stemmed from knowing exactly who had ended his brother's life, and how senseless his murder had been. If there was any doubt as to whether the cross-town Constanzio family had been responsible for Juan's death, the lipstick message on Hector's apartment patio door had clarified it.

Angelina es no limitacion

Translated, the message meant "Angelina is off limits."

Juan had always been an instant favorite among the opposite sex. His dark complexion, his six-foot, three-inch athletic frame, and the fact that he'd gone through puberty at age eleven had always made him a standout. He had hair on his chest, an impressive goatee, and pronounced muscles before the rest of his peers even graduated from youth-size T-shirts.

The fact that he almost never talked to girls seemed to only increase their desire to capture his attention. Juan seemed either unaware or uninterested in the attractions he created. He was inherently shy, and despite his size and strength, a fairly gentle individual. In fact, it was Hector who had inherited the aggressive, confident swagger of their father -- a trait that had somehow skipped Juan. Juan's intimidating size and simple stare seemed to make fighting unnecessary against most foes.

The younger Hector, on the other hand, was always willing to pursue the opposite sex, or fight for his rights among his peers. Hector was the hot-blooded brother who never walked away from a challenge.

Now as Hector stood on the church stairs, watching his brother being loaded into the converted minivan that now doubled as the cemetery's hearse, his blood boiled like never before.

The final ingredient in Hector's emotional hurricane was simple frustration. He knew that simply avenging Juan's murderer could not, and would not, cause comparable pain. Unfortunately, the leader of the Constanzio family, Angelina's family, was almost dead already. He had been shot in a fluke accident at a party and had been in critical condition for the past few months. Other than to occupy a hospital bed and to give orders to his family members and business associates, he had very little life left to give. His final passing was simply a matter of when. Most had been convinced it would be before Valentine's Day, which had already passed a week ago.

The dying leader was Patalona Constanzio. He was fifty-nine years old and the father of seven children -- six boys and one girl. Angelina was the youngest in the family, a surprise who joined the clan eleven years after the sixth Constanzio was born. At seventeen, she stood five feet, ten inches tall, was model thin, and drop-dead gorgeous.

While she liked to tell her friends that she was free from the constraints of her large family, the truth was that in addition to Patalona, she had six other fathers in her life (each one of her older brothers). Her brothers were not only committed to running one of the nastiest family businesses in Los Angeles, they were also totally committed to Angelina. They spent plenty of time and plenty of money ensuring that Angelina was safe, happy, and romantically unconnected. No matter where Angelina went, there was always a set of eyes, a set of muscles, and a set of revolvers following her. She may have been a carefree teenager, but her brothers certainly were not.

DAY 5

1:45 pm -- Covington Cemetery, Whittier, California

Angelina nervously walked toward the gathering of people that surrounded the grave site. She had heard of Juan's death, and it was impossible for her to believe that it wasn't connected to her weekend fling. She and Juan had spent the night at the beach -- first at a makeshift beach fire they had built under the Santa Monica Pier and later in the backseat of Juan's 1997 Honda Accord.

It was by no means love, but it was by no means cheap or nasty either. She knew her brothers kept a close eye on her, but she had no idea how protective they could be either -- until now.

As she approached the grave-site gathering, she was apprehensive. Had Juan told his friends and family about her? Would any of them suspect that her family was involved in Juan's death?

She was relieved when no one even looked her way as she joined the group. All eyes were focused on the casket, which was bracketed just above the open plot, and the speaker who stood next to it. The casket was simple wood, with square corners and exposed hinges and nails. Angelina was a bit ashamed of herself for instantly thinking how cheap the casket must have been. She knew that was shallow and unimportant, but for some reason her mind always completed a price inventory for every situation she encountered.

The group of fifty or so mourners was very quiet and focused as they listened to the speaker, who stood with one hand on the casket and one hand over his heart. Angelina assumed that this speaker was related to Juan, as he had the same dark complexion and strong facial features. He also had the same Mexican-American accent that she and Juan had laughed about a few nights before as he had tried, unsuccessfully, to pronounce her last name.

He spoke with passion about Juan, and the leadership he had provided in his life. As she listened to his stories, Angelina was now certain that this was Juan's younger and more vocal brother. Her heart ached to think her involvement with Juan may have somehow created this outcome.

As Juan's brother spoke, his tone changed from passion, to pain, to anger. His words seemed to get louder, shorter, and more directed at some unknown enemy. He ended his eulogy with a simple, direct, and unwavering statement; and while everything he'd said up to that point had been in English, this final phrase was in Spanish -- and no one struggled to understand its meaning:

"Mi hermano, no termina aquí!"
(My brother, it doesn't end here!)

DAY 5

Tuesday, 2:15 pm -- Mission Hospital, Los Angeles, California

The three oldest Constanzio boys stood at the foot of their father's hospital bed. He looked exactly the same as he had for the past three months -- extremely pale, extremely weak, and painfully still. Patalona Constanzio, or Papa as he was known to virtually everyone who knew him, hadn't moved even an inch in the entire fifteen minutes since his sons had arrived.

All three boys knew Papa well enough to know this was a bad sign. Papa was completely predictable, and one thing each family member knew for certain -- the madder Papa got, the more still he became.

It had been nearly one hundred days since the senseless shooting had placed Papa in such critical condition. Despite Papa's long life of violence and crime-related activities, his injuries had nothing to do with his unique lifestyle. The shootings were simply part of a family celebration, where too much drinking had led to joyous shots fired into the air at 2:00 am. The family had simply been drunk and was blowing off steam after another successful business year. To this day, no one knew which brother's bullet had cut into Papa's back -- only that a bullet had ricocheted off a stainless steel electrical box, located halfway up a telephone pole near Papa's backyard, and hit Papa between the third and fourth vertebrae in his neck. The bullet had entered through the back of the neck, ripped through his left lung, and finally lodged in his spleen. The doctors had considered removing the bullet, but X-rays and MRI analysis showed clearly that the damage was beyond repair, and in fact, removing the bullet would only further damage his mutilated spleen.

Since the accident, Papa's spleen had been slowly leaking poisonous waste into his body, and other than to fight the poisons with a

21

continuous IV drip, the doctors admitted that Papa's eventual passing was not something they could alter. Most had believed Papa wouldn't live for more than a couple of weeks, but now almost one hundred days later, Papa did what he had done for sixty-one years -- defy the odds and beat death.

"What does it mean when I say scare someone?" Papa murmured in a voice so faint that only the trained ear could recognize.

All three boys stared back at their father, but none said a word or even made a movement.

"Scare someone," Papa said, and rested before delivering the second half of his message, "means to send a message."

Finally, Bobby, the oldest Constanzio boy, spoke up. "Papa, we understood your directions completely. Our intentions were only to scare the boy."

Papa blinked so slowly that some might have mistaken it for a short nap, but then he turned his glare directly to Bobby.

"So, you understood." Papa again stopped for another breath and winced. "You simply failed to execute my directions." Papa's message was not a question, nor was it a guess. It was a clear statement, and was laced with fatherly disappointment.

"We didn't expect him to fight back like he did," Bobby offered, now getting a bit of his confidence back. "We went to talk to him, but he quickly challenged us."

"Did he have a knife? " Papa asked.

The boys waited, as it seemed that Papa might add to this question.

"No," responded Bobby, once it was clear that Papa's question was complete.

"Did he have a gun?" Papa asked as he turned his gaze to the window, as if he could no longer bear to look at his sons.

"No." Bobby knew that further explanation would only further Papa's anger.

"Did he put your life at risk?"

The three boys now looked at the floor, rather than to their father. Papa had given a clear, simple order, and they had failed. Juan Alvarez was dead. They simply got carried away in their efforts to scare a boy away from Angelina. Papa knew that unnecessary violence usually led to more unnecessary violence. The boys had been taught at a very young age to follow what the entire family knew as Papa's SBD Principles:

Send a message. Back up your threats. Death only if your life, family, or business is at risk.

Papa continued staring out the window. He wasn't sure of the right next step, but he knew his boys had started a battle he hadn't intended to start.

DAY 5

<u>**Tuesday, 2:45 pm -- St. Margaret's Cemetery**</u>

Hector watched her walk away from the grave site. While she tried to blend into the crowd, her tall, perfect frame made it impossible for her not to stand out. She was beautiful, graceful, and refined. Hector could definitely understand how Juan would have been attracted to her -- any male, for that matter, would notice Angelina Constanzio.

Surprisingly, she had come alone -- no friends, no family. Hector's feet never left the plot where Juan's body had just been lowered, but his eyes followed Angelina's every step. The more he watched, the more irritated he became.

"How could that woman have the balls to show up here?" he said under his breath. She may have spent time with his brother, she may have slept with his brother, but that certainly didn't qualify her as a friend, or as family.

Did she not know about the lipstick message on his patio door? She must not, or how could she show her face here? Whether she knew it or not, she was the reason Juan's body now lay eight feet below the ground.

As Hector's eyes followed Angelina, his mind began building a plan. The Constanzio family certainly understood the importance of protecting family ... but so did Hector!

DAY 6

<u>**Wednesday, 11:40 am -- Superior Court of Los Angeles County**</u>

"This court is now in recess until 2:00 pm," Judge Henderson said firmly as he banged his gavel on the small pad that sat in the upper-right-hand corner of his courtroom desk.

"All stand," announced the bailiff in a low, booming voice that instantly garnered respect.

"Meet you at the Y in fifteen minutes," whispered the judge to his bailiff as he exited the courtroom via the rear door that led straight to his private chambers.

There was nothing the judge enjoyed more than his lunchtime basketball game at the downtown YMCA. It was not only the serious workout that he looked forward to but also the ninety minutes of complete escape from all the lawyers, defendants, jurors, and pressures of the bench.

As he loaded his basketball shoes into his bag and headed out the door, he high-fived his senior clerk, Helen, who probably enjoyed her two hours of freedom (away from him) as much as he enjoyed the hoops.

"Play defense, too. Don't just shoot. LA doesn't need another Kobe or Lamar Odom; we need a big man that can play defense," Helen barked as he headed for the elevator.

"If they drive to the hoop with their head down, I'll be happy to show them some capital punishment," the judge joked. "Today, I'll be the Bill Lambier of the paint."

"Careful, Bill Lambier had some big thugs to back up his dirty play. You start throwing elbows at the Y, and none of those lawyers or bailiffs will step in to cover your butt," she giggled. "They'd love to see you get laid out. It would give each of them extensions on their cases."

Helen Baggitt knew that Judge Henderson loved it when she "talked hoops." In fact, she was convinced that she probably got this cushy assignment more because of her college basketball career at Duke, than because of her law degree at UCLA; but Helen didn't care; Judge Henderson was a caring man who respected her and her staff, and that was all that mattered.

DAY 6

Wednesday, 1:15 pm -- Grand Bridge Apartments, Pico Rivera, California

Hector slowly, methodically cleaned the patio window. He had purposely left the lipstick message on the window up until this point, as a reminder to himself. He had silently committed that the message would not be erased until he had a plan in place.

Now, as he slowly sprayed Windex on the sliding glass door, he watched as the chemicals hit the dried-on lipstick and began to loosen its grip on the window. He allowed the lipstick to drip and smudge before he applied the paper towel and started to wipe up the stain.

With each circular stroke, he was more and more committed to avenging his brother's death. He cleaned the message thoroughly but was careful to leave the word Angelina on the window. He wasn't ready to remove her name just yet. Since Juan's death had started and ended with Angelina, he decided to keep her name a bit longer.

Hector stared at the letters of her name until his vision became blurry. She had entered Juan's life and changed his future forever. Then she had the nerve to visit his grave site. She needed to understand that her actions would not be forgotten.

As he stood to take one more look, he made a final pledge to himself. Yes, her name would come off, but only after Angelina understood his pain. Only after Angelina understood his loss. Only after Angelina, and her entire family, understood the true meaning of revenge.

DAY 6

Preliminary hearings are pretty simple exercises, and today's prelim, as all lawyers and judges refer to them, was no different. In a prelim, the two parties gather in front of a judge to determine if there is enough evidence to proceed to a trial.

"Case number RL 8348, State of California versus José Seneca Ramirez," echoed the bailiff from his post just below and to the right of Judge Henderson's bench.

"Are both parties present and fully accounted for?" the judge asked without taking his eyes off whatever he was reading on the desk.

"The state is present and ready to precede, your honor." The LA assistant district attorney was a human tree stump. Standing only five feet, four inches, Chris Matula was nearly as wide as he was tall. As a former competitive weight lifter, his shoulders, chest, and thighs were wider than any six-foot-man the judge had ever seen.

Chris was a no-nonsense, full-throttle attorney. Around the office, the standing joke was that half of Chris's body had been left in his mom's uterus at birth -- and the half that had never come out was the half with his patience, compassion, and sense of humor.

"As we stated in our brief, your honor, the state not only has the evidence necessary to bring these charges, but we are also quite confident that this trial will result in quick and definitive guilty verdicts on virtually every charge brought against Mr. Ramirez." Chris never took his hands from his suit pants pockets, nor did he ever make eye contact with anyone or anything, other than the tips of his freshly shined Bostonian shoes.

"And I presume the defense feels otherwise, Mr. Cleary," said the judge as he looked over his cheater half-glasses to make eye contact with the defense lawyer, Matthew Cleary.

"Your honor, not only do we refute every accusation and so-called piece of evidence that the state has brought forth, but we also believe that the charge of manslaughter is completely off base and devoid of any evidence whatsoever. We have certainly made ourselves available to Mr. Matula to discuss reasonable plea options, but none of our calls or e-mails have been returned by the DA's office." As Cleary finished his response, he turned to Matula, as if to say, "You're up."

"Mr. Matula," Henderson said, in a tone that sounded more like it was scolding than inquiring, "are you opposed to saving the state of California significant time and money while still ensuring a suitable sentence for Mr. Ramirez?" The judge tapped his glasses on the large stack of legal briefs, as if to reinforce the time and effort already wasted thus far.

Assistant District Attorney Matula continued to stare at his shoes, but the increasingly bright red spots on his neck and cheeks did little to hide his angered response.

"Your honor, Mr. Ramirez stands before you for the fourth time. The people of the great state of California deserve to see Mr. Ramirez punished to the full extent of the law." The more Assistant DA Matula spoke, the more confident and aggressive his words became. "Mr. Ramirez's victims never had the chance to discuss or bargain for their future. Why should he?"

With that final statement, Matula finally shifted his stare from his shoes directly to the defense attorney, Cleary.

"Mr. Matula," the judge started, in an almost schoolteacher-like tone, "that was a very clear and very emotional argument. Unfortunately, if you were to stop looking at the floor and glance around the courtroom, you'd see that there is no jury, no witnesses, and in fact, no audience whatsoever."

Judge Henderson took a long pause to allow his words to sink in.

"You're honor, I was," Matula started, but was immediately stopped by the judge's left hand rising in a clear, definitive stop signal.

"I'm not finished, Mr. Matula," Henderson barked as his words accompanied his sign language. "This preliminary trial will not be the time or the place for you to argue your case. It will not be the time or the place to discuss your sentencing recommendations." Again the judge paused as he slowly scanned both the prosecutor and the defendant. "You are both smart attorneys, and you certainly realize that any, and I repeat, any jury trial has risks associated with it. Beyond the obvious issues of time and money, no one can adequately predict the verdict of twelve random individuals."

With that, Judge Henderson put his cheater glasses back on and appeared to read some papers from the file. After a few painfully long seconds, he continued.

"With that said, I would highly encourage you two," the judge said as he waved his hand loosely toward both lawyers, "to take the time to at least discuss your stance on pleas."

Matula's eyes returned to his shoes while Cleary's stayed locked on the judge -- occasionally nodding with visual agreement as the judge spoke.

"If, after those discussions, an agreement cannot be reached, I will most certainly schedule time in my docket for a trial." With that, Judge Henderson turned his emotional stare directly at Matthew Cleary and continued, "As it is abundantly clear that there is significant and compelling evidence to support the charges brought by the state."

As Chris Matula stood quietly waiting for the judge to dismiss both parties, he couldn't help feeling a bit perplexed. In one simple ten-minute meeting, the judge had scolded him and supported him. He was quite clear that he expected a concerted effort to find a plea, but he had also made it clear to Cleary that he would likely allow all evidence and felt compelled to support the state's case.

Chris Matula left the court the way he often did after seeing Judge Henderson -- somewhere between frustration and respect.

DAY 7
Thursday, 4:50 pm -- Judge Henderson's Chambers

"How's it going, Kobe?" It took Judge Henderson a minute to recognize the voice of his peer and b-ball playing buddy, Judge Herbert Singleton, on the other end of his seldom-used cell phone.

"On the court or in the court?" questioned Judge Henderson.

"In the court, of course," Judge Singleton clarified, by placing definitively emphasis on the phrase in the court. "I've seen you on the court, and trust me, your basketball talent is not something I would call you about."

"That hurts, Sing," Henderson said with a laugh, "'cause I've been waiting all day for the Clippers to call. Let's face it, they need some talent."

"They need talent. What they don't need is a 49-year-old white guy with shitty knees and a habit of setting moving picks," Singleton quipped in response.

"Fair enough. Truth hurts. I guess I'll stick with the robe and gavel."

Both judges shared a hearty laugh before Judge Singleton changed the subject.

"Heard you had Ramirez again. How is our old buddy José?" There was no mistaking the sarcastic, frustrated nature of Judge Singleton's question.

"You know José: another year, another felony," replied Henderson. "I was quite clear to Half-Pipe," he said, using a nickname that Assistant District Attorney Matula had acquired among the judges for his short

31

stature and explosive personality, "that he needed to find a workable plea."

"Sick of Ramirez trials or concerned about the quality of evidence?" It was clear by Singleton's question that he, like Henderson, already assumed Ramirez was guilty; it was simply a matter of whether they could nail him in with the jury.

"Neither," replied Henderson. He let his one-word answer hang in the silence for a second before he continued. "We keep sending him away; he keeps coming back. Sometimes I wonder if I'm just one of those guys with a paddle and a string connected to a ball. I hit it, it stretches, and it bounces right back to the paddle."

"He'll kill himself sooner or later. Or better yet, some other 'regular' will do it for us, and we'll get two birds with one felony," Singleton said in a tone that was semi-joking, but still serious.

"You just wonder how many lives he'll screw up between now and then," Henderson said with the recognizable sound of twelve years of judicial fatigue.

"Hang in there, Hendo, maybe the Clippers will call before Ramirez's court date," Judge Singleton said in an effort to lighten the mood. He could tell the Judge Henderson was feeling the full weight of a weeklong workload.

"I hope so," Henderson replied, "my Nike endorsement deal requires me to play for an actual pro team."

"In that case, the Clippers don't qualify," Singleton said, laughing through every word of his response. "Team, yes; pro, I don't think so." Both laughed as they wished each other a good weekend.

Judge Henderson hung up the phone and began to slowly and methodically organize his paperwork. He placed his case folders in four stacks and then placed each set of documents in its own compartment in his oversized briefcase. It was square-shaped, leather, and had been part of his life for over twenty years.

As he loaded his briefcase, he reflected on his call with Judge Singleton -- "He'll kill himself sooner or later, or some other regular will do it for us," he remembered Singleton saying. There had to be a better way -- watching lifelong criminals torture innocent victims on their way to a predictable end was beyond frustrating, it was madness.

DAY 8

Friday, 3:55 pm -- Chevron Mini-Mart, Los Angeles, California

Hector was across the street and a full block behind Angelina. With his black Raiders hooded sweatshirt, his white Oakley shades, and his oversized iPod headphones in place, it would have been difficult for his best friends to recognize him -- let alone Angelina, who had only seen him one time, at the cemetery.

She was with two friends, and it was clear that they were in no particular hurry. Angelina was clearly texting someone on her cell phone, and the responses she was getting were creating a raucous reaction from her friends. It annoyed Hector to watch their juvenile, predictable behavior.

Type the text, show her friends, send and wait, read the response, laugh in unison.

Hector's mind raced as he thought of how this scene would make for the perfect lyrics to a rap song:

> *My brother is dead, and still you laugh.*
> *No remorse, no apology -- still you text.*
>
> *You move on, as if nothing were changed,*
> *But soon you'll realize that you'll be next.*
>
> *You'll be next, you'll understand pain.*
> *You'll be wrecked, your turn to go insane.*

At the corner of the street was a Chevron gas station, with a mini-mart store. The girls entered the mini-mart, still laughing about their text message exchanges.

Hector crossed the street and broke into a quick jog to catch up to Angelina and her friends. As he reached the front door of the mini-mart, he did a quick scan of the facility. The girls were gathered in the back of the store, by the restrooms. Hector slowly meandered the aisles, as if he were searching for the perfect candy bar or chewing gum. As usual, the girls paid zero attention to anyone around them, and as a result, Hector's presence was either not known or not important to Angelina's trio.

One of Angelina's friends was waiting for the women's restroom to become available, while the other two talked about some boy named Tomas.

"Juan is gone, and on to Tomas," Hector said in a voice only his own brain could hear.

When an oversized woman unlocked and exited the women's restroom, one of Angelina's friends was ready to enter.

"Ang, hold my cell phone for me," said the friend as she did a little one-legged dance to suggest her time to pee had long since reached an emergency stage.

"Ro, if you get a message while you're in there, I'm answerin' it," Angelina responded as she took the friend's cell phone and slid it into the back pocket of her painfully tight, low-cut jeans.

"Don't you dare, Ang," her friend warned as she quickly entered the now-vacant restroom and loudly locked the door from the inside.

Ro's warning made the two girls laugh out loud as they moved toward the fountain drink station in the mini-mart.

Just then, the Eminem song Lose Yourself sprang to life at such a decibel level that anyone in the immediate zip code could hear. Hector still had his headphones on but had turned off his iPod, enabling him to eavesdrop on the girls, so when the song shot out of the phone in Angelina's pocket, Hector nearly jumped out of his skin.

Both girls immediately looked at each other and began laughing out loud while Angelina tried to free the cell phone from her back pocket.

"Be nice, Ang," the muffled voice from behind the restroom door warned.

It took Hector a second or two to put all of this together, but it now became obvious that the Eminem song was Ro's ring tone, and when the girl in the restroom heard her phone, she knew her friends would answer.

Angelina struggled to free the thin phone from its position -- lodged between her skintight jeans pocket and a rock-hard left cheek.

She set down her half-filled Big Gulp of Diet Pepsi and her expensive iPhone to free up both hands to grab Ro's incoming call. As she brought the phone from her pocket to her face, both girls strained to see the screen so they could identify the incoming caller.

Obviously excited and satisfied with the caller's ID, the girls did a little bounce dance together and started to slide back toward the restrooms. There was no doubt the girls not only planned on answering this call, but they also wanted to do so outside the restroom door so their now-nervous friend would hear every word of the conversation.

Hector couldn't believe his luck. Sitting five feet from him was Angelina's shiny iPhone and half-filled humongous jug of Diet Pepsi. The girls had now drifted back toward the restroom doors and were completely occupied by the incoming call.

After taking a five-second scan to ensure there were no cameras installed in the corners of the mini-mart, Hector headed toward the drink station. He walked with his hip sliding along the stainless steel edge of the counter. As he reached the iPhone, he simply rolled his hand out of the pocket on his zip-up hooded sweatshirt and pinched the phone between his thumb and index finger, without slowing. He rolled the phone back into his front pocket and turned it off, without looking. He didn't want Angelina's phone to ring, or make any sound, as he exited the convenience store.

When he reached the door, he peeled his headphones back to hear if there was any commotion in the store. He smiled as he heard Angelina still talking on the phone.

"Ro asked me to speak for her. She really likes you and is too nervous to talk herself." As Angelina spoke, her friend was laughing so hard that she kept clapping her hands together, as if to applaud Angelina's performance thus far.

When Hector reached the end of the Chevron driveway, he slid his headphones back in place and clicked his iPod to "shuffle songs." He had to laugh to himself, as the song that jumped on the screen said it perfectly. As the song started, his iPod screen announced the title and group:

> *The Bitch Don't Know*
> by Flying High

DAY 8
<u>Friday, 4:20 pm -- Mission Hospital</u>

"Tell me," Papa said, as if trying to conserve each sentence to the fewest possible words.

"Juan Alvarez; twenty-two years old; pretty good kid from what I can tell." Frank Delvico was a slow and steady man, and his approach to speaking matched perfectly with his approach to life. As Papa's only brother-in-law, Frank had been close to Papa since Papa married Frank's sister nearly forty years ago.

Frank wasn't necessarily "in" the family business, via Frank's own choice, but he was one of Papa's closest confidants. Papa regularly asked Frank to collect information on people, businesses, or locations. This keep Frank out of the more dicey aspects of the business, but also kept Papa and Frank close, and enabled Papa to justify a six-figure salary to his wife's brother.

"Juan's father died a few years back -- prison fight. The kid was the oldest and took care of his younger brother, who appears to be a real handful." Frank's words were so slow and measured that you could have actually kept a consistent beat with his voice. He never wavered from his pace, no matter how important the message, or how dire the situation.

Papa took a slow, deep breath. "A real challenge?" he questioned with as few words as possible.

"Grand theft auto, age eleven; short stint at Juvee; assault, shoplifting, and drug trafficking at fourteen and fifteen. Those gave him another year of Juvee." Frank watched for a response from Papa, but he got none.

38

"Charged for attempted rape at seventeen -- got off; charged for assault and battery at eighteen -- spent eight months at Tehachapi for that one." Tehachapi was the street name for the California Correctional Institution, which was located in Tehachapi, California. Frank revealed he was finished by closing his small, pocket-sized spiral folder that he had been reading from.

Papa turned his head toward the window and closed his eyes. "Juan's record?" he asked.

"Doesn't have any priors, as far as I can tell. He's been in a few neighborhood fights, but seemed to spend most of his time trying to rehabilitate his younger brother."

Frank stayed silent. He had long ago learned that Papa's long silences were not to be broken. After at least three minutes of nothing -- no speech, no movement, no noise -- Papa returned his gaze to Frank.

"How bad?" was all Papa said. Frank understood the question completely. He was asking how bad was the beating his boys had given Juan Alvarez.

"Bad."

Papa only wanted details when details were needed. Frank's one-word answer had been a full response. Papa reached up his right hand, which had two tubes sticking out of it. Frank stepped closer and grabbed Papa's hand without a word.

"Eyes open, Frankie."

Papa then released Frank's hand and returned his gaze to the window. As usual, Papa had not asked Frank to get involved or to execute an order. He was simply asking Frank to be Papa's eyes and ears and report back any change in events as it related to the previous execution of one Juan Alvarez.

DAY 8
Friday, 4:40 pm -- Bus Route #17

After a quick jog through the alley across from the Chevron station, and four brisk blocks of speed walking, Hector hopped on the city bus that was bound for Pico Rivera. He settled himself into the last seat, in the last row, against the window and slid his headphones back off his head and around his neck.

He reached into his sweatshirt pocket and retrieved the iPhone he had swiped at the mini-mart. Along the walk to the bus, he had started to worry that maybe the phone wasn't Angelina's. Maybe she was simply holding that phone for another friend too. However, his worries were quickly erased as he examined the shiny aluminum frame and saw the personalized, etched message on the back:

My Love, My Life, My ANGel
Love, Papa

Hector couldn't help but smile from cheek to cheek. This was Angelina's phone, and Angelina was Papa's most prized possession. And possession was the right word. Papa didn't just protect his family and his business, he owned them. Papa might be dying soon, but Hector sure hoped he live long enough to feel real pain, beyond any that a gunshot wound or faulty spleen could cause.

Friday, 4:55 pm -- Los Angeles County
District Attorney's Office

"Why won't he just let me nail him to the wall?" Chris Matula asked his boss, the much more seasoned and much more respected Geoff Robbins. "We've got his nuts in a vice. You'd think Henderson would be granting me the fastest possible trial so he can hammer Ramirez in his sentencing."

Geoff Robbins loved Matula's passion. In fact, Robbins wondered if the twelve years he personally had spent on the job had caused him to lose some of the passion he had when he first got started, right out of USC Law. Matula certainly had his weaknesses, and his personality could aggravate even the most perky of clerks, paralegals, and peers, but you could not coach passion. You either have it, or you don't. Robbins was smart enough to know that and experienced enough to make sure he didn't try to beat any of that passion out of his assistant DA.

Robbins knew that most of the judges called Matula Half-Pipe, but if any of those judges were in a bind personally, they'd want a lawyer with the same persistence and the same pit-bull personality that they joked about when they discussed Chris Matula.

"Chris, before you decide what Judge Henderson should be doing for you," Robbins began, as slowly as he possibly could. Robbins had learned the best way to make Matula listen was to force him to slow way down in his dialogue. "You need to focus on the real objective for our case with Ramirez."

"Ramirez is going away for a very long time," Matula was already answering before Robbins finished his sentence.

Again Robbins paused, not because he wasn't ready to respond, but he knew Chris wasn't ready to listen.

"The good news, Chris, is that we all agree on that -- you, me, and Judge Henderson." This first statement was perfect for any discussion with Matula, because it gave him nothing to respond to.

"So, if we want to make sure Ramirez spends a long time in the shit house, and Judge Henderson agrees with us, why would he push for a plea?" As Geoff talked, he closed his eyes and slowly turned away from Matula. This was to make sure that Matula would know that any body language reaction he might have would not be important to Geoff, and to suggest he wasn't finished talking.

"Judge Henderson has seen Ramirez in his court multiple times. In those cases, he has been found guilty for various crimes and has been sentenced harshly by Henderson, right?" Geoff turned to Matula for confirmation.

"Yep," Matula replied, still not sure he was following where Robbins' comments would lead.

"But Ramirez keeps coming back, and Henderson keeps spending weeks reading briefs, reviewing legal precedent, and supervising trials for this repeat, repeat offender." Robbins took a quick sip of seriously stale coffee and continued.

"So here's the question, Chris. What's the difference between you pleaing out a ten-year sentence or you completing a full trial with Henderson providing a sentence?" Robbins asked somewhat rhetorically and somewhat directly to Matula.

"The difference is seven or eight years," Matula said, impressed with himself on the brief but factual response.

"The real difference?" Robbins shot back with a clear emphasis on the word real.

"I don't follow," Matula admitted.

"That's right, you don't follow. You don't see what really happens, because you only focus on the conviction and the sentence -- and you're done." Robbins' pace was quicker now as he was giving his pupil, Matula, the real lesson for the day.

"Judge Henderson sees the real outcome. The difference between your plea sentence and your full-scale trial sentence, in actuality, is a couple of years. If you get him fifteen years from a jury conviction, he'll serve seven. If you plea out to ten, he'll serve five. Judge Henderson has been around long enough to see the real difference."

Robbins wrapped up his point by saying, "The real difference is minimal. Either way, Henderson gets to see Ramirez in five to seven years, when he commits an even more heinous crime."

Matula did what he rarely ever did -- he sat quietly. He hated the fact that Robbins was right, and hated even more that a judge might be encouraging him to plea, simply because two to three years of additional jail time just wasn't worth the effort.

"That sucks," was all Matula could muster.

"It may suck, Chris, but it's reality," stated Robbins. "The judge hopes that you, me, and this department spend our time on more pressing issues than two years, give or take, on a "regular.'"

"Why can't we push to put him away for longer, right now?" Matula asked, even though he already knew the answer.

"Ramirez won't go away forever until he steps further over the line, and we all know he will in time. Trust me, Judge Henderson knows it too; but for now, we can only address the crime at hand."

With that Robbins got up and started to leave Matula's office as if to say "Glad we had this talk, hope you learned something." When Robbins got to the doorway, he made one final statement, without turning around for confirmation: "Let me know where you net out on that plea."

DAY 8

<u>**Friday, 6:35 pm -- Outback Steakhouse,**</u>
<u>**Montebello, California**</u>

Frank was getting a little worried as he waited for his bloomin' onion and peppercorn steak to be delivered. When he had left Papa at the hospital, he had sent a text message to Angelina.

A couple of things you could always count on with Angelina -- she'd never answer her phone if her dad, brothers, or Frank called, but she'd always return a text message. Frank was always blown away with just how fast she would respond.

Frank hated text messages. For one thing, his phone was about four generations behind current technology and didn't have a full keyboard -- meaning if Frank wanted to type the letter c, he would have to press the number 2 three times. If he mistakenly pressed it more than three times, which Frank almost always did, he'd have to keep pressing it, to go through a full array of symbols, capital letters. Secondly, Frank had big hands and thick fingers. While the kids always told him to "just use your thumbs," Frank's thumbs could never have just one key. So for Frank, sending a text was harder than actually typing a letter the old-fashioned way on a typewriter. Text messages were just another modern convenience that he wished had never been invented.

His text to Angelina, which read "call me – F" had taken him five minutes to type, not to mention the time it took for him to make capital F. Frank had expected a text back from Ang before he left the hospital parking lot, but when he arrived at Outback Steakhouse for his favorite Friday meal, he was surprised that he still had no response.

After he sat down, he did his best teenage impression when he texted Angelina another short message:

U OK?

44

He hoped his short, letters-only text would get a chuckle out of Ang and a quick response -- but still nothing.

Frank called Bobby, the oldest Constanzio boy, to check in.

"Baa-bee, it's Frank," he started.

"Yo, Frank -- how's Papa?" Typical of Bobby, as he always knew when and where everybody in the family had been.

"He's okay, I guess. No real change -- good or bad." Frank figured Bobby was getting hourly reports from the doctors and any visitor Papa might have, but he was glad Bobby asked him too.

"Bobby, I was trying to track down Ang. Have you seen her around today?" Frank wanted his question to seem as nonchalant as possible. No reason to worry Bobby because of slow text responses.

"She's with Ro and Darci. After school they went shopping, and then they were going to a movie after that." Once again, Bobby's personal GPS on the entire family was alive and well. "She's probably got the cell turned off in the theater. You need me to get a message to her, Uncle Frank?"

"No, it's not that important. I was just saying hi more than anything. If you see her this weekend, have her give me a shout. No hurry." Frank knew Bobby would see Angelina ten times or so over the next two days, so he wasn't too worried about Ang.

"Will do, Frank. Outback again tonight, or headin' home?" Bobby asked.

"Peppercorn and bloomin' onion," Frank said, laughing in reply. Damn, that kid is good, Frank thought.

Bobby pressed "End" on his cell phone to terminate the call and quickly shot a text message to Angelina.

A, call me

It wasn't like Frank to call Angelina a lot, and if Frank wasn't getting through, that was even more strange. Probably nothing, Bobby thought, but I'll feel better in a minute or two when she calls back.

DAY 8

Friday, 7:15 pm -- Grand Bridge Apartments, Pico Rivera, California

Damn, does that thing ever stop buzzin? Hector thought as he watched the slender phone shake and shuffle across his bedroom dresser, as it vibrated with every incoming message. It had been receiving a steady stream of messages since he turned it on during his bus ride home. Only one call, which Hector had sent to voice mail, but plenty of text messages, he thought.

He grabbed the phone and hit "view messages" to see what had come in since he'd hopped in the shower when he got home. As Hector looked at the string of messages, he couldn't help but laugh out loud.

5:19 PM from Ro
If you found my phone, could you please call this number, so I can get it back.
Thanks, iPhone owner
310-459-9493

5:21 PM from Tomas
Call me - T

5:46 PM from Tomas
?? - come on!

5:54 PM from Tomas
If u r goin 2nite - call

6:08 PM from Uncle F
Call me - F

6:14 PM from Dee Dee
Where r u

6:19 PM from Tomas
Don't be a bitch - ?

6:27 PM from Uncle F
Y OK?

6:31 PM missed call – Bobby
Voice mail

6:51 PM from Dee Dee
R u goin 2nite? I M!

7:04 PM from Dee Dee
Mt u there 9.5

7:08 PM from Bobby
A, Call!

"Sorry, Tomas, Bobby, Frank, and Dee Dee, but Angelina is a little out of touch this evening," Hector said out loud as he sat alone in his apartment bedroom. "But maybe I can be of some assistance," he said with a laugh.

With that, Hector opened the first text, hit reply, and started communicating to all those who had sent a note:

8:04 PM to Tomas
Yea - I M goin

8:04 PM to Uncle F
Sorry, low battery. Will call tomorrow

8:05 PM to Bobby
Low batt - what need?

8:05 PM to Dee Dee
Where r u goin?

He laid back on his pillows and waited. He knew it was only a matter of minutes before he'd hear back from each one of them.

He was right:

8:07 PM from Dee Dee
Fri fun nite. Oyster Park. 9:30

8:08 PM from Bobby
Just ckn in, call latr

8:11 PM from Uncle F
Where are u?

8:14 PM from Tomas
Meet b4?

Hector couldn't believe how easy this was going to be. He typed out his final messages and started to plan his night.

8:17 PM to Bobby
OK

8:19 PM to Uncle F
With Ro. Talk tomorrow.

8:20 PM to Tomas
Just meet @ Pk

8:20 PM to Dee Dee
C u there 9

DAY 8
Friday, 6:35 pm -- Pico Rivera Village Walk Theatres

Officer Dennis Patrick, or D-Pat as he was called by nearly everyone who knew him, heard the click at first and then saw the light. His automatic headlights had just kicked in, confirming that daytime was over, and evening had officially begun. It made him laugh, but that simple little click, that slight illumination of his dashboard, meant so much more in his line of work.

Daytime was a great time to be a cop -- kids were excited to say "hi," store owners routinely voiced their appreciation, and soccer moms waved enthusiastically during the daytime patrol. D-Pat had to admit that the life of a daytime patrol cop felt a little bit like being a rock star -- everybody looked, everybody respected, and some would even go out of their way just to thank you for the job you did.

But as daylight faded and sunglasses gave way to headlights and streetlights, there was no mistaking the metamorphosis that happened with police officers. Friendly waves vanished at nighttime, as soccer moms headed home and store owners closed their shops.

Nighttime brought with it a heightened tension for any cop. Perhaps it was the inability to see other drivers, or the fact that 80 percent of burglaries, murders, and accidents happened after dark. Regardless of the reason, nighttime meant tension, no doubt about it.

Dennis' Friday evening patrols were always different, but they always had three things in common. Dennis made a mental note to be a Friday night regular in three local hot spots -- the huge multiplex Village Walk Theatres the outdoor mall, and Oyster Regional Park. All three were favorites of the local high school kids. Dennis wasn't really out to arrest teenage kids on a Friday night; in fact, just the opposite. Despite the fact that he had entered his thirties on his last birthday, he still could remember the joys of high school life, and he personally believed that every kid should experience the freedom, the fearlessness, and excitement of that age. He tended to over-patrol these areas, according to his patrol sergeant, but Dennis didn't care. Dennis knew that any location that attracted large gatherings of teenagers needed a more consistent police presence, and at least as long as he was on shift, he intended to be that presence.

As he slowly rolled his police cruiser through the parking lot of the megaplex theatres, it was clear that most movies were just about to start. The outside ticket window was down to four or five customers, but just inside the huge glass doors, the lobby was wall-to-wall kids -- scrambling to get their last concession stand purchase before the coming attractions.

Small groups of girls and boys were dangerously sprinting through the parking lot, obviously late and trying to get to their movie on time. Like all teenagers, they were completely oblivious to anyone or anything around them, including an occasional police squad car.

Dennis made three painfully slow passes in front of the theater, with the third one being greeted by an appreciative wave by the theater manager. Feeling confident that everything was as normal as it could be for a Friday night at the movies, he headed to the main exit to make his way over to the mall -- hangout number two for groups of excited teenagers.

DAY 8

Friday, 8:47 pm -- Grand Bridge Apartments

Hector still couldn't believe how opportunity had literally fallen into his lap. The cell phone at the mini-mart, Dee Dee's text confirming Angelina's plans for the night -- Oyster Park, 9:30, Friday Fun Night -- and the etched inscription and Angelina's phone from her father, Papa.

Hector couldn't believe how easy this had been. While he had never been a big church guy or serious believer in God, he had always wondered about the afterlife. Were his parents together again in some form of heaven? There had to be something, anything, more than just nothing when life came to an end.

Now, as Hector reviewed the dumb luck that he had experienced all day, he was starting to wonder if there wasn't some truth to one of his brother's favorite sayings -- "There's no such thing as a coincidence." He started to believe that maybe, just maybe, his older brother, Juan, was still guiding him.

Juan had always been there to provide support and direction. When he was alive, Juan would never tell Hector exactly what to do, mostly because he knew Hector would fight against any direct orders. No, Juan would simply provide suggestions and subtle reminders that would allow Hector to believe he was making his own decisions.

It was hard to argue with today's incredible coincidences. One thing was certain: if Juan was watching, he was certainly approving of Hector's plan of revenge.

Hector's mind snapped back to the present situation as he grabbed Angelina's iPhone and retrieved the first text message he had saved. He reread the message, as he pondered his next move.

<u>5:19 PM from Ro</u>
If you found my phone, could you please call
this number,
so I can get it back. Thanks, iPhone owner
310-549-9493

Hector laughed to himself as he thought of Angelina's text. No
abbreviated words, no funny text codes. She typed out every word
and used proper punctuation. She hadn't expected some kid to have it.
She was hoping it would be a trusted adult, who would simply return
her property. Well, thought Hector:

<u>8:47 PM to Ro</u>
I have it. Found it at the gas station.
Was going to turn into the police, but
I'm glad you sent this. How can I return
it to you?

Hector hit send and awaited the response that he knew would come
in a matter of seconds.

<u>8:48 PM from Ro</u>
Thank you! Thank you!
I'll come get it, where are u?

Hector smiled. Angelina couldn't help herself -- she got so excited,
that she quickly typed u, instead of the full word you.

<u>8:50 PM to Ro</u>
I'm just about to leave for
the evening. Any chance you
live East of LA?
If not can we exchange tomorrow?

There was no way Angelina, or even Ro for that matter, would wait
a full night to get back her precious little link to life. He chuckled to
himself as he imagined Ro and Angelina on the other end, retrieving
his text. He envisioned a perfect little "valley girl" scene -- the two
of them doing their hair and comparing makeup tips, in between
hundreds of text messages. He could almost hear their words:

"Oh, my, God! He's even going to be on the east side, Ang. We'll just get it before O-Park."

Hector's humorous daydream was interrupted by the sound of an incoming text:

> 8:51 PM from Ro
> Yes. I'll be at oyster park.
> How can I get it from you?
> Just say where/when?

Hector smiled as he typed -- this sounds about as old, white, male, and boring as I can be, he thought to himself.

> 8:53 PM to Ro
> I'll call the number you gave
> me at about 10 PM, when I'm
> going by oyster park, and we can
> meet - okay?

> 8:54 PM from Ro
> Great - thank you!
> The number is my friend Ro,
> but I'll be with her tonight.

Hector quickly typed his final text response:

> 8:57 PM to Ro
> See you then

On his bed he began to lay out his materials for the night. Starting with clothing, he set out black jeans and all-black T-shirt. Then, using a kitchen chair as a ladder, he brought down an orange Nike shoe box from the top shelf of his bedroom closet. As he carefully placed the shoe box on his bed, he removed the contents he needed:

One nine-millimeter black Beretta pistol

One Vanguard drop-point hunting knife with leather belt holder

One Taser C2 stun gun

Two plastic baggies filled with heavy-duty zip ties
(the kind usually associated with reinforcing chain-
link fences or securing heavy tarps over a pickup
truck payload)

One two-inch-wide roll of industrial-strength silver
duct tape

No one knew about his special Nike shoe box stash -- not his brother,
not his friends. Hector was certainly no stranger to breaking the law,
and as a result, he understood that preparation was a key ingredient
to success.

After he got dressed, he loaded the Beretta and placed it in the front
pocket of his baggy black jeans. Next he wove the leather knife holder
through his belt. Finally, he stuck five or six zip ties in between his
belt and his jeans. As he pulled his belt tight, it firmly held the zip
ties in a vertical position. Before fastening his belt, he slid one end
through the circular role of duct tape. Then he when secured his
belt, it not only held his knife, but it also tightened around the zip ties
and the roll of tape. He decided to put the C2 Taser gun in the glove
compartment of his car, but everything else he needed was now neatly
located within his grasp.

Hector took a long look in the mirror. His heart was already beating
at twice its normal rate, and despite his mind-over-matter breathing
techniques to try to calm down, he was already beginning to sweat,
like a runner just before a big race.

"I love you, Juan," he said aloud as he locked eye contact with his
reflection in mirror. "I can't bring you back, my brother, but I can
send you some company."

With that, Hector grabbed the Taser gun from the bed, grabbed the
car keys from his bedroom dresser, and headed to the door.

"Nunca se olvida," he said with purpose as he walked out the door,
which specifically translated means never forgotten.

DAY 8

Friday, 9:45 pm -- Oyster Regional Park, Los Angeles, California

As Angelina and Ro pulled into Oyster Park, they would never have known they were being watched. Their heads were racing with thoughts of Friday Fun Night and meeting up with Tomas and all their other friends from school. But as they left their car in the parking lot, and started moving toward the main sidewalk that led into the park, their every step was being observed.

Just across the parking lot was a toddler playground area that was completely vacant, and completely dark, at this time of night. Of course, the play area had all the basics -- swings, rocking horses mounted on massive metal springs, and jungle gym bars. The ground was covered with a soft layer of oversized wood chips. But like any good play area, it also had a central structure -- the main piece of equipment. In the case of Oyster Park's playground, it was a big metal structure that was designed to look like a rocket ship sitting on a launching pad. It had large red wooden panels on the exterior that surrounded the three stories of metal stairs hidden within. It also had two slides that extended from small openings at different levels of the rocket's internal stairs. At the very top of the rocket was a small metal platform that was designed to comfortably fit the bodies of two or three toddlers who were daring enough to climb all the way to the top.

While it was really just a children's playground, the view from the top platform of this rocket was the best in the park. From this unique vantage point, one could see all the paths, entrances, and wooded areas that Oyster Park had to offer.

That's why Hector had chosen the rocket ship for his base. He could not only see Angelina and Ro as they parked their car and headed into the park, but he could also see the small gathering of friends about five hundred yards away that was likely their final destination.

Hector grabbed the iPhone and typed in the first step of his plan:

> 9:50 PM to Ro
> **Should be by park soon.**
> **Can we still exchange?**

Hector sat with anticipation as he waited for his text to reach Ro's phone. Angelina had just started down the sidewalk that would pass through a small wooded area of about fifty yards before exiting into a large grassy area that would separate them from their group.

He saw both girls stop and look at Ro's hands. He was certain Ro had received the text, and true to their habits at the mini-mart, they were reviewing it together. While his message created no visible reaction from either girl, Ro handed her phone to Angelina, who was obviously typing a response. After thirty seconds or so, Angelina returned the phone to Ro, and both girls stood motionless, awaiting a response.

> 9:52 PM from Ro
> **Yes. Where?**

Short and sweet, Hector thought. She's getting anxious; so much for the long, punctuated notes.

As Hector looked up to reconnect visually with the twosome, he saw another set of girls coming toward them from the parking lot. There were three girls in this group, and they appeared to be roughly the same age. Like Ro and Angelina, they were clearly excited to get to their final destination, as they were literally bouncing down the path.

Hector stayed perfectly still in his rocket perch as he watched the set of three girls move along the path toward Ro and Angelina. Because of the solid black, moonless night and the fact that Oyster Park had virtually no lights, the two groups got about ten feet apart before they were able to get a good look at one another. At that point, both sets of girls erupted in screams and giggles.

"No way," said the loudest of the group.

Because of the chaos of voices, Hector only got parts of the conversation, but phrases like "just got here," "those are great," and "me too" convinced him that they were close friends and excited to be joining each other for Friday Fun Night -- whatever that was.

As the full group of five turned and started walking through the wooded path, Hector decided to strike again:

9:58 PM to Ro
**Can you meet me on the
street - next to the toddler
play area? I'll be in a green Lexus.**

Green Lexus was a good touch, Hector thought, complimenting himself. Lexus was generally an older, safer car, and nobody young and scary would ever be caught dead in a green-colored Lexus.

Now Hector waited as he watched for the reaction. Three of the girls had started a kind of half jog, half dance in what looked like an effort to get to the party faster. Unfortunately, Hector couldn't tell who was who. Suddenly, the three girls who were in a hurry stopped. Hector saw one of the girls hold up her hand and yell back to the other two. As much as he strained, he couldn't hear what she said.

Then four of the girls continued down the path toward the party, while one turned and walked back, at an impressive pace, toward the parking lot and play area.

Hector assumed that Ro had received the text and yelled back to Angelina, to tell her he was coming to the street by the play area. He assumed it was Angelina who was coming back, but with the dark surroundings and still one hundred yards or so separating them, he couldn't be sure.

Hector slid down into the base of the rocket-shaped staircase and peered out the opening to one of the slides. If Angelina was the one coming back, then Juan was still watching over him -- because she was not only alone and completely removed from her friends, but she also suspected nothing.

DAY 8
Friday, 9:25 pm -- Morongo Resort and Casino, Cabazon, California

Bobby's hands nervously stacked and restacked the poker chips that were neatly aligned in front of him. He kept telling himself to focus on the poker game and the body language of the players at his table. He knew from experience that poker was never won with the luck of the cards, but rather with mental superiority. From an early age, he had trained himself to study the mannerisms of his competitors so that he could catch even the slightest amount of nervousness, confidence, or confusion.

The best part about playing in the Morongo Gold Club was that only serious, accomplished players participated. To enter this room, and take one of the six available seats, it required a fifty-thousand-dollar upfront buy in, at least three previous experiences at the "Red Carpet Level" (where a twenty-five-thousand-dollar buy in was mandated), and an agreement to stay in the room for no less than two hours. Unfortunately for Bobby, it also required all players to leave their cell phones, pagers, BlackBerries, and any other metal devices in a locker in the reception room. The Gold Club was for serious players -- the kind that prioritized the game ahead of anything else in their lives.

Most of the time, Bobby was a huge fan of every Gold Club rule -- it was this no-interruption, poker-only focus that drew Bobby to Morongo every Friday evening. It was a quick fifty-mile drive from LA, and it allowed Bobby to get his competitive fill for the week before he was forced to spend the weekend with his wife and kids -- chauffeuring children to youth sports and dance recitals.

Unfortunately, tonight's game was different. Bobby had shot a text to Angelina at 7:00 that had taken her almost a full hour to return. When she did respond, she claimed to have a low battery. While neither the slow turnaround time, nor the low battery was typical of his iPhone-addicted younger sister, Bobby had figured she was okay and entered the Gold Room to start his night. At 8:30, he gave his BlackBerry and Bluetooth earpiece to the three-hundred-pound pit boss who managed the lockers for all Gold players. The pit boss looked like a combination of NFL offensive lineman, and the famous Indian from that pollution commercial that used to air in the 1970s. He had twin braids that ran down each one of his enormous shoulders, and his face never showed emotion. His sport coat must have been a size 58 or 60, and still it pulled at the seams of his arms, chest, and neck. Bobby had heard that he was a chief in the Morongo tribe, and although he said very little, his words were much respected among his tribe.

Now, as every minute of his two-hour minimum went by, Bobby was more and more convinced that he'd made a mistake. Even if Ang had gone to a movie, she would simply have turned her cell phone to "vibrate" and continued sending and receiving text messages throughout the show. In addition, Ang would never let her battery get below even 50 percent. She couldn't live without that shiny little connection to her puberty-driven friends.

The more Bobby thought about the text exchange they'd had, the more nervous he became. He had already lost twenty-two thousand dollars, and with his mind racing about Angelina, it wasn't likely to get any better.

The clock over the doorway read 9:57, and he wouldn't reach his two-hour limit until 10:30.

"Shit, twenty-three more minutes," Bobby said to himself.

She's probably just fine, he kept saying over and over in his head, but he couldn't make himself believe it. If she was in trouble, he'd never forgive himself for waiting twenty-three more minutes simply to save his fifty-thousand-dollar buy-in fee.

Before he could once again talk himself out of it, Bobby stood up abruptly. "I'm out," he said without any hesitation or apology.

"Mr. Constanzio, the dealer hasn't even finished dealing this hand," said the Indian pit boss, who was standing motionless by the door.

"How can you know you are out if you haven't even seen your hand?"

"I don't mean I'm out of this hand," Bobby said, clarifying his statement. "I'm out of this game. I have to go." Bobby looked around the table to gauge the reaction of his competitors, but each of them had already turned their gaze to the Indian pit boss.

"Sit down, Mr. Constanzio," said the Indian, with the same emotion you'd get from a postal worker at tax time.

"Trust me, it's an emergency. I think my track record will support that I am not someone that breaks the rules of the club; but tonight, I simply must go." Bobby tried to make his words sound as official, and as final as he could.

"You know that you will forfeit your entire entry fee, and you will not be allowed in a Gold Club game ever again," the chief said, not as a question, but as a simple fact.

"Understood." Bobby really wanted to question the ban from the Gold Club, but he figured this was neither the place nor the person to have that discussion with. He needed to confirm that Angelina was okay, and to do that, he needed to get to his BlackBerry immediately.

"Gentlemen, Mr. Constanzio's chips will be distributed among each of you, based on the amount of chips you have currently. In order to do this, please slide back slightly from the table, and our dealer will divide out his chips." There was a noticeable change in the room as the disposition of the players went from frustrated to relieved. "Mr. Constanzio, please follow me, and your personal items will be returned to you."

Bobby followed the massive Indian out the door, and back to the reception area that housed the lockers for each player. He apologized again to the stoic pit boss as he retrieved his personal items, but the chief either didn't care or simply didn't respond to any of Bobby's comments. Once Bobby had all his items, he left the room and quickly walked back to the main ballroom of the casino. Turning his phone and Bluetooth earpiece back on, he dialed Uncle Frank's number.

"Baa-Beee," Frank answered in his very customary way.

"Uncle Frank," Bobby said, trying to talk slowly and conceal the panic that was beginning to bubble out. "I've got a bad feeling about Ang. She did shoot me a text saying she had a low battery, but the more I think about it, the more I know that Ang would never have a low battery on a Friday night." As Bobby talked, the pace of his dialogue got faster, despite his desire to slow down. "We've got to get in touch with her. I'm going to try to call, but will you make a trip to the Village Walk Theatres, Uncle Frank?"

"If you're worried, than I am worried," Uncle Frank admitted. "I'll leave right now. Where are you going to go?"

"If I remember right, Papa told me there's a way to track Ang's cell phone," Bobby said as he tried desperately to remember the conversation he had had with Papa about Angelina's phone. "Evidently, it has some sort of GPS tracking within it, but I'll have to find someone that can show me how to find it."

Bobby headed for the parking lot in a half walk, half jog. His gut wasn't always right, but it was right more than it was wrong. If his gut was right tonight, he was already too late.

DAY 8
Friday, 10:05 pm -- Oyster Regional Park

Hector did a quick mental check of his inventory of weapons, as the shadowy teenager moved closer to the play area. In his front pocket Hector had the loaded Beretta pistol, which he hoped to never use, as the loud noise and proximity of Angelina's Friday Fun Night friends would make a clean escape nearly impossible.

Connected to his belt loop on his right hip was a brand-new hunting knife, with a nasty serrated edge. Hector wasn't sure if his target would understand the severity of this item, given how dark the park was at 10:00 pm, but there was no doubt in Hector's mind that the knife would cause the most lasting wounds, if he was forced to use it. On his left hip, sandwiched between his belt and jeans were six heavy plastic zip ties. No different from a set of police handcuffs, Hector knew that those ties had the strength to bind any human, in any situation. Also lodged between his belt and jeans was a two-inch-thick roll of duct tape. Lastly, in his left hand Hector squeezed the C2 Taser gun that he'd stolen in a recent neighborhood fight. While he'd never used a Taser gun himself, he'd certainly witnessed its impact.

As the lone teenager approached the playground area, there was now no doubt that it was Angelina. Hector was instantly reminded of both her beauty and her height. At five feet ten inches, she was a stunning figure, and Hector realized that she might be able to put up more of a fight than he anticipated.

Angelina was clearly scanning the area for the green Lexus, and because of that, would have never considered the danger that lingered in the playground. However, the quickest way to the street was through the wood chip area and right past the large rocket structure.

As she crossed under the swing sets and through the jungle gym, Hector felt a unique combination of sexual arousal and heightened fear. He reached down to shift the revolver to his back pocket, for fear that his now rock-hard penis was too close to his gun.

Angelina stepped about five feet from the rocket on her direct path to the street. Hector was quick and accurate as he sprung from the inside of the rocket and lodged the Taser into Angelina's back right shoulder blade. She was only able to produce a muffled gasp, as she quickly sucked her lungs full of air. However, her sound was quickly muffled as Hector shot three hundred thousand volts of electricity through her startled body.

The Taser made an eerie electrical buzz, as if it had caught a mosquito in a bug zapper. The electrical probes that fired the voltage from side to side gave off a second-long flash of light, which startled Hector more than either the Taser's sound or Angelina's reaction.

Angelina's body went limp almost immediately. First, her knees caved forward, as if they'd been kicked from behind. Her arms drooped, and her head swung forward, burying her chin into her chest. Once her knees hit the wood chip floor, the rest of her body toppled forward, with her face creating the final collision with the ground.

Hector, who was startled himself by both the electrical zap and the quick flash of light, lay on the ground next to Angelina and listened for any commotion in the park. After a few painfully long seconds of virtual silence, Hector rolled Angelina over and got to work.

He took off her shoes, put her feet together, and grabbed a zip tie from under his belt to bind her ankles together. Then he took out his hunting knife with his right hand and cut off Angelina's skirt and panties in two perfectly clean cuts. It felt like he was cutting the plastic bands that sometimes accompany a well-wrapped package. The fabric in her clothing put up some resistance, but with the sharpness of the blade and Hector's aggressive motion, they simply gave way to the knife.

Hector unfastened his belt, which freed the duct tape he had pinched between it and his jeans. When he found the edge of the tape, he pulled away about two feet from the roll. Kneeling down, he lifted Angelina's unconscious head and placed the starting point of the tape on her right cheek. With an amazingly steady hand, he directed the tape over her mouth and around the back of her head. Initially, he was frustrated as the tape got caught up in Angelina's long dark hair, but as he pulled hard on the tape roll and circled her head, he felt the adhesive grab.

He left the nose uncovered, so that she could still breathe, but to ensure she couldn't make a sound, he continued to cover her mouth multiple times. He probably would have been fine with two or three wraps around her head, but in his panic and anxiety to make sure the tape would hold, he ended up using the entire roll. As he inspected his final work, Angelina had roughly a one-half-inch layer of duct tape over her mouth and chin.

With her mouth covered and feet secured, Hector now pulled her arms back behind her body to bind her wrists with zip tie number two. With the same fury and precision placement, Hector cut Angelina's blouse -- reaching up under her shirt to start his blade at her neck and tearing the fabric right down to her waist. Removing the cut blouse from her still-limp body, Hector was both surprised and sexually aroused by the fact that Angelina was not wearing a bra.

With all of her clothing removed, Hector returned the knife to its holster and reached into his sock to remove a small silver container he had brought for just this purpose. He pulled the top off the container and twisted the bottom, causing red lipstick to pop out of its cylindrical base.

To this point, all of Hector's moves had been quick, violent, and aggressive, but as he leaned over Angelina to leave this important message, his movement became slow and exact. As he slowly spelled out his lipstick rebuttal on Angelina's tanned, and perfectly conditioned back, Hector wished he could see Papa's stunned reaction when he found his ANGel.

DAY 8
Friday, 9:50 pm -- Oyster Regional Park

While there was no such thing as a typical Friday night in his line of work, Officer Dennis Patrick was experiencing a pretty routine shift. He already had made a couple of swings through the theater parking lot, made one quick pass by the mall, and had stopped two teenagers and one very agitated businessman for moving violations.

He was pulling out of a corner 7-Eleven, where he had stopped for coffee, and was now planning on finding a quiet place to finish up the paperwork on the three citations he had written. He headed north to Oyster Park, as he figured he could achieve two objectives with one stop. He liked to visit the park a couple of times a night, given the propensity of teenage kids to hang out in the park's wooded areas; and secondly, he could use the quiet parking lot at Oyster to complete his paperwork.

As he slowly entered the park, he was immediately reminded of just how dark this property became at night. There always seemed to be some parent group lobbying the City Council to add lights in the park, but the homeowners association of the neighborhood surrounding the park had formed a pretty strong coalition over the years and had successfully fought any lights being erected. They were convinced that bright lights would not only lower their property values, but also encourage even more kids, drug dealers, and vagrants to use the park after hours.

Funny, D-Pat thought, as he slowed his car to an idle crawl, these neighborhood watch groups never understood the basic rule of teenagers. Putting up a few lights in this park would not only make it safer for the local residents, but it would also thin out the high school crowd. Kids don't like to illuminate their hangouts.

DAY 8

Friday, 10:10 pm --Oyster Regional Park

Hector had now completed the basics of his plan. Angelina was unconscious, gagged by enough duct tape to harness a horse, and bound at the hands and feet. In addition, Angelina's back now showcased the perfect response to both Juan's death and the patio window warning.

He stood up on the wood-chip surface and inspected his work. He gathered up the empty cardboard roll that had housed the duct tape, and the three extra Ziploc ties that had fallen when he unfastened his belt. He also gathered Angelina's shirt, panties, and blouse and put them in the black pull-string bag that had held that the Taser gun.

He set the bag at the base of the metal rocket ship and returned to Angelina's body. His original plan had been to carry her into the nearby wooded area, only seventy-five yards or so away, but he now realized that she was heavier than he had planned. She had almost zero body fat, at least that was visible to Hector, but her five-foot ten-inch frame simply weighed more than Hector had bargained for.

He quickly looked around the play area and saw a metal grid, displaying a tic-tac-toe board. It was built with a metal frame that outlined nine square-shaped boards that swiveled on hinges. The structure stood about four feet high and three feet wide, was cemented into the ground, and probably was designed for kids to throw beanbags or balls to expose an X or O for each box.

Hector stared at the small metal wall and decided that based on its weight, strength, and proximity to Angelina's now-unconscious body, it would work perfectly. He carefully lifted Angelina around the waist, with her back toward his face. He was careful not to smudge his prized lipstick message as he dragged her toward the metal grid with her feet and face skimming along the wood chips. When he reached the four-foot-high metal wall, he lifted hard to get her waist up and over the top bar of the structure.

Her face banged against the wooden X and O plates as he positioned her face down on the unit. Her legs were now on one side of the structure, and her head was on the other. Hector was proud of himself for the improvisation in using the structure and doing it with almost no noticeable sounds.

He ran back to the black bag that held all the items and retrieved two remaining zip ties and the Taser gun. Returning to Angelina, he set the Taser on the wood chips and reached for his hunting knife. Almost without effort, he severed the zip tie that held Angelina's ankles together, and put the now-broken zip tie in his front pocket. Hector then pulled her legs apart and put one leg on the far left side of the structure and one leg on the far right. With two of the unused zip ties he had left, he bound Angelina's ankles to the bottom tic-tac-toe squares -- forcing her legs apart. With her waist at the top of the metal structure, her upper body dangling over the metal wall, and her feet bound to the opposite, lower ends of the metal grid, Angelina's perfectly sculpted, naked butt was now facing Hector.

As he stopped to look at his shackled victim, Angelina started to make a barely audible, groggy whimper. She was clearly regaining consciousness, but at a very slow pace. She lifted her head up slightly, pulling her face away from the tic-tac-toe grid. Just as she began to arch her back in an effort to pull her upper torso away from the metal wall, Hector reengaged the metal needles of the Taser gun into the back of Angelina's neck. Identical to its first use, the C2 Taser sprang to life with a combination of an electrical zap and short burst of light. In less than a second, Angelina's brief bout with consciousness was over, as her body immediately went limp once again. Her face swung forward and once again came to rest against the wooden plates.

The second Taser shot had been much less of a surprise to Hector, and as a result, neither the sound nor the brief flash of light deterred him from his focused actions. With Angelina once again strung over the metal wall in a lifeless fashion, Hector returned to his initial plans.

While the moves that Hector had made up until this point had been about Juan and revenge for his death, Hector now had to admit that his current state of sexual arousal and his desire to overpower Angelina's now-lifeless body was driven more from his own desire than that of revenge. Hector's mind slipped into a tunnel-vision state, and all he saw was Angelina's naked, inviting body. As sweat poured down his face, from both his physical efforts to bind her and his heightened sense of arousal, Hector lowered his pants and boxers to his knees and moved to Angelina to leave his final message.

DAY 8
Friday, 10:21 pm -- Orchard Outdoor Mall,
Pico Rivera, California

Frank could feel his cell phone vibrating, but since it was in his right front pocket, which was now trapped under his fastened seat belt, he couldn't get to it in time. He usually wore one of those nerdy belt-clip phone holders, but tonight when he'd received Bobby's call and requests to see if Ang was at the theaters, he'd simply tossed it in his pocket and bolted out the door.

Frustrated and annoyed, Frank pulled his Lincoln Town Car into a gas station, unstrapped his seat belt, and retrieved his phone. The external window on his phone told him what he already expected:

1 - missed call - Bobby

Frank flipped open his phone and hit the send button, which automatically dialed the number of his missed call. Without ringing, the call went directly to Bobby's voice mail, which told Frank Bobby was talking on the other line.

"Probably leaving me a message right now," Frank thought to himself. He flipped his phone shut, set it in the cup holder next to his arm rest, and refastened his belt. He knew if Bobby called him back, he'd be able to grab it now, and if it vibrated in that plastic cup holder, it would make enough noise to capture his attention.

Before Frank could shift into drive, the phone was rattling in the holder. Frank flipped it open, and before he could say "hello," Bobby was already talking -- or perhaps yelling was a better description.

"Frank, it's Bobby," he said in a hurried, nervous voice. "Ang is at Oyster Park, or maybe just outside the park."

"Did you talk to her?" Frank asked, instantly relieved that Bobby had located her.

"No! She still doesn't answer. I had someone track her location, and she's been in the same spot since he first tracked it, which was about fifteen minutes ago." Bobby was so out of breath that it was hard for Frank to decipher every word.

"Where are you, Frank?" Bobby asked.

Frank knew Bobby was both serious and nervous, as he'd only called him Frank, without the "uncle" precursor, a couple of times that Frank could remember.

"At the mall. Didn't see Ang at the Village Walk Theatres, so figured she might be over here," Frank said, explaining why he wasn't where Bobby had initially requested.

"I can get to Oyster Park in about fifteen minutes," Frank said, figuring it was about ten miles of traffic-light driving.

"I'm about fifteen minutes away too," Bobby said as he checked his navigation screen, which was set to Oyster Park. It said he was twenty-three minutes from his destination, but at the speed he was driving, he was likely to cut that time in half.

"I'll meet you at the main entrance," Frank said.

"If you get there first, don't wait for me -- find her," Bobby said. It was the first time that Bobby's voice revealed the pure panic he was feeling.

Frank got the hint and provided the most comforting response he could think of.

"We'll find her, Bobby. She'll be fine."

Frank flipped his phone shut, and for the first time that night, he wondered if Angelina was in serious trouble. Papa, in his very simple and proud way, had asked Frank to keep her safe. As Frank sped to Oyster Regional Park, he prayed he hadn't let Papa down.

DAY 8
Friday, 10:23 pm -- Oyster Regional Park

Dennis slowly trolled the winding entrance of the park. He had turned off all his lights and lowered his front two windows, as he had learned early in his career that sounds can give kids away, but lights give cops away.

He noticed four or five cars in the parking lot, all of which looked like the kind of first-car beater that teenage kids in this area would drive. As D-Pat approached the parking lot entrance, he heard what sounded like a blown electrical fuse box, or maybe even a high-powered bug zapper. He eased down on the brake to bring his patrol car to a stop and listened for it again -- but nothing.

Then Dennis heard rustling just to his left, at the toddler playground. He knew the surface was lined with wood chips, and it sounded like someone was walking slowly, or dragging their feet, on the splintered surface.

Dennis turned his window-mounted spotlight toward the playground and threw the switch. The police-caliber spot immediately flooded the area with 5.5 amps of brilliant light. The instant visual scared Dennis as much as it did the person he now illuminated. Dennis was stunned to see a medium height Hispanic male with his pants around his knees, a fully erect penis, and some kind of metal object in his right hand. Immediately in front of the man was a completely naked person who was fully bent over a short wall, with his or her stomach and head on one side and legs on the other.

Dennis's initial thought was that he had just interrupted a gay encounter, and while he knew it was illegal to be completing this act in a public park, he hated that he had caused this kind of personal embarrassment.

Unfortunately, Dennis' initial prediction was erased almost as quickly as it formed, as the Hispanic male tugged upward on his pants with his left hand and tried to run as fast as he could. Surprisingly, the man's partner, who was caught in the most exposed position over the wall, remained completely still.

Dennis left his floodlight on the scene and immediately jumped out of the car to begin pursuit on foot. As his jog became more pronounced into a full-on sprint, Dennis reached up with his right hand and pushed the button on his patrol microphone, which was attached to the left shoulder of his uniform.

"Unit 413 in need of backup," Dennis said in between quick breaths. "Oyster Regional Park!"

As he reached the play area, Dennis could see that the body bent over this small metal wall was that of a tall female, and that her ankles were bound to the base of the metal poles.

"Oyster Park. Toddler playground parking lot," he barked, loud enough for the person who was tied the poles to hear.

"Are you okay, ma'am?" Dennis said, as he approached the lifeless body.

When he received no response or reaction to his question, Dennis reached out to touch one of her bound wrists. He was relieved to discover that she not only had a pulse, but it appeared to be quite strong. He wasn't sure why she was so nonresponsive, but he assumed significant drugs or alcohol were involved.

"413, in Oyster Park, now!" Dennis barked as loud as he could into his microphone. There was clearly both adrenaline and fear in his voice, as he now realized that he was all alone in a dark park with at least four cars of people somewhere in the immediate area.

A loud thud refocused his attention, as the Hispanic male who had fled the scene had gotten tangled in his own pants and had hit the ground about thirty yards away. Dennis saw him struggle to pull the pants from his knees and get back to his feet at the same time.

As fast as he could move, Denis turned and sprinted straight toward the male suspect. He knew that if this suspect were to get to his feet and correct his current pants dilemma, Dennis would likely never see him again. The fall had given Dennis his only opportunity to track him down.

The male had his back to Dennis, so he couldn't see him coming, but his movements were quick, panic driven, and clumsy. Dennis figured the suspect knew his time to escape was limited.

In an effort to correct his pants, the suspect, who was dressed in all black, had dropped his weapon (or whatever he was carrying) on the ground next to him. Dennis saw him reach down to retrieve it just as he looked back and caught a glimpse of Dennis.

With ten yards separating them, and without slowing down, Dennis put his right hand on the holster of his police-issued, nine-millimeter Glock and shouted, "Freeze, police!"

Dennis realized that if this guy was able to secure his weapon in the next second, he might have an open shot at him. Without thinking it through, Dennis sprung from his feet in a full-body dive toward the suspect's chest. In a tackle that would've made any NFL highlight film, Dennis hit the suspect square in the chest, just as he turned to face him. The impact sent both bodies airborne about five feet. Dennis heard the same disturbing electrical crackle as he made contact with the suspect. Luckily, Dennis's weight advantage and his clear momentum advantage resulted in Dennis landing directly on top of the Hispanic male suspect. He heard the nauseating thud as the victim's head slammed back into the turf as Dennis' weight planted them both into the sod.

As Dennis reached out to secure the suspect with his left hand, he noticed the Taser gun on the ground just above the suspect's head. He reached out and grabbed the Taser gun and tossed it as far as he could over his shoulder.

"Don't give me a reason, shithead," Dennis said as the adrenaline and emotion of the moment poured out of his mouth. "You're under arrest, and if you so much as move, I'll beat you lifeless." Dennis was not simply sending a message. He had every intention of backing up his threat if this suspect gave him any trouble.

The Hispanic male suspect was clearly dazed by the tackle and the subsequent violent head snap into the ground. Dennis could see that his eyes were fluttering, and while he wasn't sure if that was drug related or head trauma related, he knew that if he hurried, he'd be able to cuff and corral the suspect himself.

As he pinned the young suspect to the ground, with his left hand firmly wrapped around the boy's neck, Dennis reached back to retrieve his police-issued handcuffs. He was relieved to hear the sound of screaming police sirens in the background as sweat rolled off his chin and onto the suspect's face.

"You have the right to remain silent," Dennis began, "and I'd strongly suggest you utilize that right."

As Dennis finished reading the Miranda rights to his freshly cuffed suspect, he couldn't help but cringe. This lowlife couldn't have been more than eighteen or nineteen years old, and he was moments away from changing the life of a young girl about the same age. As Dennis dragged the suspect back to the playground surface, it occurred to him that this young kid was probably going to spend the next eighteen or nineteen years of his life behind bars.

DAY 8
<u>10:59 pm -- Oyster Regional Park</u>

Bobby's stomach tightened so hard that he almost regurgitated his dinner. As he exited Interstate 605 and bulleted down the service roads toward Oyster Park, he heard the sound he least wanted to hear.

It was clearly more than just one siren, because the cadence of the audible wails seemed to overlap one another, resulting in a kind of consistent, garbled alarm. As Bobby turned right and headed for the main entrance to the park, he saw the distinctive circular flash of blue lights, which told him police were on the scene.

"Please, God," Bobby said aloud to himself, "let it be silly kids stuff." Drugs, drinking, having sex -- he could deal with the stupid things kids tend to do.

Bobby turned into the main gate but only got about fifty yards down the main entrance before he saw the roadblock. Two police squad cars were facing each other, perpendicular to the road, causing an automotive wall on the entrance parkway.

Bobby could see three police cars up ahead by the main parking lot and a small gathering of people just on the opposite side of the lot, near the children's play area.

"Son of a bitch," Bobby said as he hit the steering wheel with his right hand. "Five cops and an ambulance cannot be good news," he murmured to himself.

He swung his car around in a complete U-turn to park along the side of the entrance. It was then that he noticed Frank's "whale," as the Constanzio family had come to call the Lincoln Town Car. Bobby must have looked right past it as he drove in, distracted by the overwhelming police scene.

Bobby parked two cars in front of the whale and quickly got out. He raced back to Frank but saw that his car was dark and empty. Bobby now had lost all ability to stay under control, and in a dead sprint, he headed to the gathering of people and police.

As Bobby reached the parking lot, he saw the ambulance turn on its lights and sirens, adding to the already-deafening noise and visual chaos. The ambulance pulled through the parking lot and then went over the curb and through the grass in an effort to avoid the police car barricade that blocked its departure. Once it was past the cop cars, it returned to the pavement and headed for the park exit. Bobby couldn't help but notice that the ambulance was not moving fast -- it didn't appear to be in a race to save someone's life. In fact, in Bobby's experience, that type of ambulance pace meant the life was likely already lost.

As Bobby turned to watch the ambulance leave, he felt a hand on his shoulder. The surprising contact, combined with Bobby's already jittery nerves, made him jump in response.

"Bobby," Frank said, now reaching up with his other hand so that he had both of Bobby's shoulders secured in his two hands. "Bobby, it's me."

"Uncle Frank?" Bobby said.

Frank quickly thought how Bobby was becoming a lot more like Papa every day. He now asked one hundred questions in just two words -- was she here; was she all right; have you seen her; is she hurt? All the questions poured out of Bobby's frightened face.

"She's okay, Bobby." Frank figured he'd better start slow.

"Where?" Bobby responded, almost as if he'd never heard Frank's reassurance.

"She's going to the hospital to get checked out," Frank began, "but the paramedics say she appears to be unhurt."

"What the fuck does that mean?" Bobby said only hearing the words hospital and hurt.

"Bobby, listen to me," Frank said in the slow, methodical way that only Frank could.

"Someone tried to hurt her. But," Frank paused, allowing Bobby to keep up with his words, "the police caught the guy before he got to her."

"What guy ... where is he?" Bobby said, and then before Frank could respond, he added, "What hospital, Frank?"

"She was tied to one of the playground toys and apparently hit with a Taser gun, maybe more than once." Frank could see Bob was about to explode with more questions, so he put up his hand to tell Bobby to stop and let him finish.

"Cops don't know the kid. He had no ID," Frank continued, "but they caught him with all his weapons, his pants at his knees, and nowhere to run." As Frank talked in his steady pace, he left his hand up, as if to suggest to Bobby that he would lower it when he was completely finished.

"She was clearly frightened and a little woozy, but she appeared to be unhurt physically." Frank lowered his hand.

"Tell me about the guy they caught," Bobby said, gritting his teeth as he talked.

"All I heard the cops say was young, male, Hispanic. They may know more, but they weren't going to tell me," Frank replied.

"I know him," Bobby said, looking over his shoulder as if he was mapping out a route to the kid's house that very moment.

"Hospital, Frank?" Bobby asked, in a tone that said "right now."

"Mission." Frank knew Bobby had heard enough.

"Fuck," Bobby yelled as he turned and jogged toward his car. Both Frank and Bobby knew that Mission Hospital was the same place Papa was located.

DAYS 9 – 22

NO REGRETS ... NO DEALS

DAY 9

<u>Saturday, 2:05 am -- Mission Hospital</u>

Dennis stood on one side of the hospital bed, with Detective Felix Bernard on the other. Angelina was between them on the bed, under a paper-thin blue hospital blanket. She looked remarkably well, despite the evening she had just experienced. Her eyes were red and puffy, likely a result of excessive crying, and she had small red dots covering her cheeks and chin. Dennis assumed the facial marks were a result of the layers of tape that she had around her face when he found her in the park.

It must have been painful to tear all that adhesive from her face, but as Officer Patrick and Detective Bernard stood next to her, she gave no indication of discomfort. She simply stared straight ahead and seemed oblivious to their presence.

While Angelina's brother had been quite aggressive in his desire to keep cops and detectives away from Angelina's bedside, Detective Bernard was not deterred and pressed to talk with both the arresting officer and the victim before the next morning.

It'd been a long night for everyone, and as he stood in the hospital room, Dennis could smell his own body odor. He still had dirt in his hair, and his shoulder ached from his body slam in the park.

Angelina was perfectly still and continued to look down at her feet, making eye contact with no one. Dennis feared this was a post-rape trauma, which often causes the victim to feel shame, despite the fact that she is the one who has been victimized, but her lack of dialogue made it difficult to be sure.

"Officer, can you spell your last name for me," Detective Felix Bernard started.

"P-A-T-R-I-C-K," Dennis responded with a hint of a laugh, as no one had ever struggled with the spelling of Patrick before.

"And you were the first officer on the scene?" the detective asked.

"Yes, and the only officer, until after the arrest was made," Dennis said, quite proud of his single-handed arrest.

"Can you tell me the position of the suspect when you arrived?" Bernard continued, in a monotone, emotionless voice.

Dennis glanced down at Angelina, because he didn't want to upset her anymore. He hoped Detective Bernard would catch his visual cue and move to another question, but it was clear that Bernard was waiting for a response.

"He was about a foot away from Miss Constanzio," Dennis offered.

"Did he appear to be stepping away from her, or stepping closer, when he spotted you?"

"I'm not sure. He was clearly startled when I hit him with my floodlight. That clearly caught him by surprise," Dennis said, trying to paint a complete picture for the detective without reliving it for Angelina.

"Was he in physical contact with Miss Constanzio?" Bernard asked, as if Angelina wasn't even in the room.

"Not when I saw him," Dennis answered quickly.

"What was he doing when you," Bernard said, reflecting back on his written notes from their discussion thus far, "hit him with your floodlight?"

"His pants were lowered, and he was clearly aroused," Dennis said, almost whispering the final words of his statement.

"He did have a Taser in his hand at the time," Dennis added as he recollected the park scene.

"Miss Constanzio, did the suspect touch you in any way? Did he say suggestive things to you?" Bernard said as he directed his first question to Angelina.

Angelina's expression never changed, and it appeared that she hadn't heard him at all.

"Miss Constanzio," Bernard said, wondering if she was not able to comprehend the question.

"I have no idea what he did," Angelina whispered in a voice so slight that it was barely audible.

"Excuse me, ma'am," Bernard said, as he clearly hadn't understood her response.

"I have no idea what he did," Angelina said as she turned and stared directly at Felix Bernard for the first time. "I have no idea what he said, or what he did to me."

Angelina continued her stare, waiting for some response. Then she added, "He could have done anything, but I don't remember."

As she said her final words, Angelina's body curled up in a ball, like a small child trying to stay warm.

DAY 11
<u>Monday, 9:35 am -- Superior Court of Los Angeles County</u>

As he opened the case file, Judge Henderson was delighted to see the final plea agreement that had been written by Matula and signed by all the relevant parties. He knew that he shouldn't find joy in this outcome, but shamefully, that was the exact emotion he was feeling as he quickly added his formal approval by signing the agreement.

He was proud that Half-Pipe had heeded his advice and spared the court another long-winded Ramirez trial. The ten years that both sides had agreed to would probably only result in five or six years of time served, but Judge Henderson wasn't sure if they would have done much better with a jury trial.

Pushing the record button on his handheld Dictaphone device, he asked Helen to call Assistant DA Matula's office, on his behalf, and say that he was pleased and impressed by the speedy outcome. He had to admit that while Half-Pipe Matula could really be a pain in the butt, his heart and his passion were good for the DA's office.

He put his head back on his oversized leather chair and sighed. "Another day, another 'regular' heading off to prison," he said aloud to himself.

Helen stuck her head in the door. "Prelim at 10:30, hoops at 11:45, and the Ramirez plea is in your top folder. Other than that, you should have some downtime this afternoon. Maybe you can finally learn how to rebound this afternoon," she said with a giggle.

"Yeah, I'm reading the Ramirez plea right now. Call Matula to say nice work, or remind me to do it this afternoon," the judge said, preempting his dictation note.

"Got it. You okay?" Helen said, noticing that the judge was in his head-back thinking position when she stopped in.

"There ought to be an office pool to guess how many years it will be until we see Ramirez again. You know, like those Super Bowl parties where everyone gets a square. Just a matter of time before he kills someone," the judge said, talking more to himself than to Helen.

Monday, 10:35 am -- Los Angeles District Attorney's Office

Monday mornings were always the most hectic but also the most interesting day on the job. At the District Attorney's office, Monday meant sorting out all the new case files that had come in over the weekend. The majority of drug deals, domestic violence, DUIs, and gang shootings seemed to take place on Fridays or Saturdays, so Monday was like drawing straws at the DA's office. Everyone got at least one new file, and you never knew what it was going to be.

As Chris Matula sat in his boss' staff meeting, he knew it was only a matter of time before his superior, Geoff Robbins, distributed the results of this past weekend's activities. Robbins had already reviewed the department's new travel policy guidelines and discussed the new procedure on filing cold cases, so he was running out of political BS to discuss.

"Okay, gang, that just leaves us with new files for distribution," said Robbins as he turned to the pile of green legal-sized hanging folders that had been stacked in front of him the entire meeting. Matula was sure that every one of the four assistant district attorneys in the room had been focused on that stack of files since the meeting had begun.

"Julie," Robbins said as he turned to Julie McPherson, who was the newest member of the team. She was legally brilliant, based on her law review, with a serious overachiever's resume, but still a little timid in the courtroom. As a result, Robbins was clearly handing her the softer cases.

"You've got an assault and battery, probably gang related; kicked the shit out of a guy at a dry cleaners." As Robbins handed her the file, he finished with his standard line, "Get me a one pager by Friday."

Robbins always wanted a brief summary of the case before any assistant district attorney got too deep so that he could quickly drop the weak cases and keep his team focused on the most relevant issues.

"Matula, you've got attempted rape," Robbins said, obviously not giving Chris the same first-name treatment he had just given to Julie. Chris didn't care. He knew he had Robbins' respect, and that was evident by the quality of caseload that Robbins consistently assigned to him.

"Constanzio family member, Oyster Regional Park; you should nail this quickly," Robbins directed. He was clearly telling Chris not to waste time, but rather to plea-and-go.

"One of the Constanzio boys caught in a rape?" Chris tried to sound as perplexed as he felt. "They'll lawyer up big time," Chris responded, knowing that Papa Constanzio protected his own, and money was never an issue.

"Not the Constanzio boys," Robbins shot back, "the girl. She was an attempted rape victim."

Chris' mind was racing. "I didn't even know there was a Constanzio girl."

"There is, and now she's essentially your client," Robbins said as he handed Chris the green file and patted him on the shoulder. "One pager, by Friday."

DAY 11
Monday, 11:25 am -- LA County Jail

Hector's request for an ice pack had been denied. His head was still throbbing, and a very substantial bump had formed just behind his ear. Hector didn't remember the specific collision that had caused it but assumed it was a result of his head snapping back into the turf when he was tackled by the cop.

The last sixty hours had been a combination of physical pain and mental anxiety. Physically, his wrists were still cut and bruised from the aggressive handcuffing on Friday night. Hector had tried to use his own saliva to remove the dried blood that surrounded the sharp cuts on each wrist; but now, two days later, it still looked like he had stains in his skin. He assumed the reddish-yellow color was a combination of some internal bleeding and deep tissue bruising. Mentally, he was feeling a bit lost. With nothing to do but sit and think, Hector realized that for the first time, he truly had no one to help him.

For all Hector's life, Juan had been his guiding light and his safety net; and while this wasn't the first time Hector had experienced jail, it was the first time without Juan waiting to help him out.

No one had talked to him since the night he was brought here. He had been given the opportunity to make a phone call, about 4:00 am on Saturday morning, but Hector had refused. Who was he going to call?

The longer he sat in this temporary lockup facility, the more he became convinced that prison was actually his best option. He hated the idea of being locked up with no freedom -- but if he was truly honest with himself, the idea of trying to live his life "on the outside" without Juan was just as unsettling.

He had learned the last time that he had returned from California Correctional Institution, that there were no legitimate job opportunities for a young man with a prison record. He could either cut grass all day long or sell grass all day long. The first paid roughly six dollars per hour, and the second paid as much at six thousand dollars per month, but tended to lead right back to prison in Tehachapi.

As he continued to try to rub the bloodstains from his wrists, he knew that his future was already predetermined. He'd be spending the next forty to fifty years of his life in jail, or doing something that would return him to jail.

Juan had given him so many chances to change his life and straighten out his ways. Now Hector was convinced that he was out of chances.

DAY 12

Tuesday, 1:15 am -- Los Angeles District Attorney's Office

"Chris, there's an Officer Patrick on line two," Jenny said as she leaned back in her chair from her cubicle in order to make eye contact with her boss, Assistant District Attorney Chris Matula.

Chris put his hand over the mouthpiece section of his phone and whispered back, "I need to take that. Give me ten seconds to lose this one." Chris had been anxious to talk to Dennis Patrick since reading his crime report earlier Monday morning.

"Felix, I gotta call you back. I'm sorry, but I've got a live one on the other line," Matula said, in an effort to quickly end the call he had just started with Detective Felix Bernard. Chris knew he'd need to spend some quality time with Detective Bernard, but reaching patrol cops was never an easy task, and this case really started and ended with Officer Patrick.

When Chris replaced the receiver, he immediately yelled out to Jenny.

"Ready for him."

Jenny had already set the line to auto forward, so Chris' phone started ringing as soon as he got the words out.

"Officer Patrick, this is Assistant DA Chris Matula," he said, avoiding the standard "hello" and "how are you" greeting.

"Yes sir, I'm returning your call," said Dennis. He was at his kitchen table reading the LA Times article regarding the attempted rape at Oyster Regional Park. No names were given, for the suspect or the victim, but D-Pat was surprised at just how accurate the reporter's version had been. Amazing they can get it so right with virtually no witnesses other than himself, D-Pat thought. Sure, those teenagers came out of the woodwork, after all the sirens and ambulance, but none actually witnessed anything.

"I read your crime report regarding the rape at Oyster Park," Matula began, "and I was hoping I could fill in some more blanks by talking with you."

"Mr. Matula, that has to be the fastest anyone has ever read one of my reports. I didn't even file the final copy until late Sunday night." Dennis had never been called regarding a crime report, and to be completely honest, he doubted whether anyone ever read them all the way through.

"Yeah, this one got a little special attention, for a lot of reasons," Matula chuckled. "Constanzio is a big name; Alvarez is no stranger to our judicial system; and residents of Oyster Regional Park are not shy when it comes to protecting their little plot of Los Angeles County."

Matula believed all three reasons were valid, but his desire to provide a complete outline to Robbins by Friday was probably the overriding force.

"Didn't know she was a Constanzio until after I got to the hospital," Dennis admitted.

"Officer, can you give me the sixty-second overview of the scene when you arrived? I know you've written the whole thing up, but sometimes hearing about it paints a clearer picture for me."

"Sure," Dennis began, "it's pretty simply, really."

Dennis closed his eyes and let his mind drift back to Friday night's arrest. His captain had always preached "BFB" when recounting an event for the courts -- brief, factual, and brief. The captain usually took the liberty to change the meaning to "be fucking brief" when he was reiterating his point to a longer-winded colleague.

"I heard an electrical sound and some rustling as I cruised past the toddler play area in the park. When I hit the area with my floodlight, I caught him pretty much in the act." Dennis took a break, as he could feel himself launching into a full-out story, and not necessarily following the BFB principle.

"Explain the term electrical sound," Matula asked during Dennis' pause.

"Like an electrical short, or even like a bug zapper," Dennis said, hearing the distinctive buzz in his head.

"Thanks, please continue," Matula encouraged.

"Well, when I lit up the scene, the suspect was standing with his pants down, his pecker up, and a Taser in his hand," Dennis said matter-of-factly, and then paused for effect.

Matula started to ask a question but caught himself. Better to just let him flow, he thought.

"The suspect was about a foot or so away from the vic, who was bound to a small metal play structure," Dennis continued. "Actually, her ankles were bound to the base of the structure, and her wrists were bound behind her back, but she was bent completely over, face forward."

"I'm not sure I follow," Matula lied, in an attempt to get Officer Patrick to provide more detail.

"She was face down, and she was bent at the waist -- legs on one side of this little metal wall, top half on the other," Dennis explained. "She was completely naked, and she was unresponsive."

"How'd you know she was unresponsive?" Chris pondered.

"Hey, Mr. Matula," Dennis said in a much more informal voice, "to be honest, when I lit up the scene, I thought I'd just frightened a couple of homos, or a couple of kids gettin' freaky on a Saturday night."

"How do you know you didn't?" Chris shot back almost immediately.

"A few pretty simple clues," Dennis chuckled. "One, the suspect had a Taser gun. Two, the girl that was hooked to the little wall was completely unconscious. Three, there was a fairly distinguishable mark on the vic's back," Dennis said, as if to encourage Matula to ask about it.

"Yes, I read that in your report. What was that all about?" Matula asked.

"On her naked back, written in lipstick, was a little message. Not sure who was the intended reader," Dennis admitted.

"How do you know the suspect wrote it?" Matula once again, asked the question more to keep Officer Patrick talking than to hear a specific answer.

"Don't know for sure," Dennis said, sticking to the actual facts, "but we found a lipstick container that matched the color in the suspect's sock. Pretty sure it will match when we see the lab work."

"How do you interpret the actual message, officer?" Matula asked, as that was probably the number one reason Chris had called Officer Patrick in the first place.

"I'm no detective, Mr. Matula," Dennis said, being careful to keep it brief and factual, "so I'm not sure I can help you with that."

"How exactly did it read, Officer Patrick?" Chris asked, even though it was clearly identified in the crime report.

"Just like I said in the report -- all capital letters, very neat," Dennis shot back. "It simply said, NO LIMITS."

DAY 12

Tuesday, 12:55 pm -- Los Angeles Downtown YMCA

"Hendo, either you're poppin' a serious amount of Aleve, or those knees are feeling better," Judge Singleton said as he dressed in the men's YMCA locker room.

"Sometimes they're good," Judge Henderson replied, massaging his knees with his thumbs, "and sometimes they're bone on bone."

"I like playing against you better on bone-on-bone days." Judge Singleton laughed as he closed his locker and began packing his gym bag with his sweaty clothes.

"Did you see Hector Alvarez is coming back?" Singleton added.

"What do you mean 'coming back'?" Henderson questioned.

"Hendo, don't you read the papers anymore, or is the sports section all you can handle?"

"What the hell are you talking about, Sing? I read The Times every day. You know that," Henderson shot back.

"Oyster Park last Friday night," Singleton explained, "they busted a kid who had a young girl strapped to some playground apparatus."

"Yeah, I read that," Judge Henderson interrupted, to stop his buddy from retelling the entire story.

"Well, turns out the rapist was Hector Alvarez." As Judge Singleton talked, he was clearly watching for some reaction from his buddy. "The same Hector Alvarez that you and I both put in Juvee, and you sent to Tehachapi," Singleton said, hoping to jog his memory about their sentences on juvenile detention and prison.

"The name rings a bell," Henderson said, obviously unable to place the face.

"His rap sheet will ring it loud and clear for you," his buddy fired back. "You'll recognize the kid the minute he steps in your courtroom."

"Here's the kicker," Judge Singleton continued, "the girl that he had shackled to the playground was only seventeen years old."

"Oh, shit," Henderson said, thinking about his own twenty-year-old college sophomore.

After a long silent spell between both men, Judge Singleton zipped up his gym bag and slapped his friend on the back as he headed for the door with one final comment:

"Another day, another regular."

DAY 13
<u>Wednesday, 8:19 am -- Grand Bridge Apartments</u>

"Well, I think we can scratch off one of our preliminary questions," Detective Felix Bernard said to his new and very junior partner, Campbell Warner.

Campbell was not only twenty-six years old, but she had recently been promoted to junior detective after only two years of patrol duty. Bernard had to admit that she was as smart as anyone he had ever met, but like most truly gifted academics, she lacked basic common sense.

"What question is that?" Campbell said, before really thinking about Detective Bernard's comments and the obvious clue that they had just uncovered. Almost before the words left her mouth, she wished she could take them back. She knew she was talented enough to be in this position within the police force, but she also knew that young, blonde, and female meant there were plenty of rumors in the department about how she'd "been given" the job, rather than how she'd earned it. Because of that, she knew that any airhead comments, like the one she'd just made, would quickly make it back to the office and fuel the fire.

"Campbell, did you not see the patio window?" Bernard's question clearly carried a degree of disgust, as he pointed to the sliding glass, patio door in Hector's apartment.

"That glass looks amazingly clean everywhere except the area where Angelina's name is written," Bernard continued, as if the first comment was never made.

Campbell was a little embarrassed, but she followed Bernard's lead and focused on the window's cleanliness. With a long look at the sliding glass door, she saw what Detective Bernard was quicker to notice. The window actually looked as if it had been recently cleaned, and

97

probably on both sides. However, there was a noticeable circle of dust and smoggy film that encircled the lipstick word that was written on the window.

"We can cross off whether or not this was a random sex act in the park," Bernard said, returning to his original point. "He obviously targeted Angelina Constanzio, and Oyster Park just turned out to be the place where he attacked."

"You are right, Felix," Campbell said as she knelt down to take a closer look at the patio window, "this window has definitely been cleaned all around her name."

"Why the lipstick? Would a guy really use lipstick, even if he had a sexual hangup with the vic?" Bernard wondered aloud, hoping Campbell would somehow have a better handle on how a young male might think.

"Maybe she wrote it," Campbell considered out loud. "I could see a young girl leaving a lipstick message."

Bernard looked up and closed his eyes to give the appearance of deep thought. "Do you think she's tied to his brother, Juan, in some way? Or do you think Hector and Angelina may have had some sort of preexisting relationship?"

"The girl we saw at the hospital," Campbell said, referring to the meeting that Felix had with Angelina and the arresting officer early Saturday morning. Campbell had considered joining in the hospital room, to provide Angelina a female face, but later decided to simply stand in the hallway to limit the number of people asking her questions at such a tender stage. "That girl didn't act like she'd had a fight with a boyfriend, or had known her attacker at all," Campbell continued. "Remind me, what happened to Hector's brother?"

"His body was found in a dumpster behind an In-N-Out Burger. He was beaten badly, and apparently one of the blows to the head put his lights out on a permanent basis," Bernard recounted.

"Can't be a coincidence that Hector's brother gets snuffed out, and then Hector goes hunting for Angelina Constanzio, right?" Campbell wanted to prove that she followed Bernard's line of thinking, but she wasn't sure she understood any clear connections, just yet.

"No way these things are unrelated," he agreed. "But why rape her? And why do so in a fairly public place? He had a knife and a gun on him, but if he was going to kill her, that's a strange location to choose -- a park filled with her friends."

"Some would say that rape is more personal than simply murdering her." Campbell was again thinking out loud.

"So is leaving a lipstick message on her back," Bernard said, agreeing with his young apprentice.

DAY 13
<u>Wednesday, 2:40 pm -- Mission Hospital</u>

Angelina slowly opened the door to Papa's room but didn't step in. She could see that his face was turned away toward the windows, and as such, she couldn't tell if he was awake. The two large electrical machines, which were connected to Papa's internal organs, were lit up like dashboards in a Boeing jet. A series of green and yellow lights were flashing every couple of seconds, recording a pulse rate, blood pressure, and all types of other measures that Angelina didn't understand.

"Come in, Ang," Papa said without turning his head or moving an inch. "I'm not asleep, and I'm not dead yet."

Angelina wasn't surprised a bit that Papa knew it was her without looking. The truth was, she couldn't remember a time when he didn't have that unique gift.

She walked slowly, carefully to his bedside and took a seat in the lone leather chair, which some previous visitor had obviously moved closer to his bed. She'd been released on Saturday afternoon and had been at her brother Bobby's house ever since. Bobby had asked her several times to go see Papa, but until now she simply hadn't been able to move.

"You all right?" Papa said, still looking away.

Angelina said nothing, but reached out and grabbed Papa's white, withered hand. He returned her squeeze with surprising strength and held it firm as if to avoid being the first to let go.

"Ang, you okay?" Papa turned to face his only daughter and revealed the swollen, red, puffy eyes and noticeable tracks of tears on his cheeks.

Angelina had never seen Papa cry -- not one single time. The visual stunned her and perhaps caused as much personal pain, and shame, as any she'd felt in the park.

"I'm so sorry, Papa," she said in a very soft whisper.

"Ang," Papa said with a deep, struggling breath, "you've only brought me joy." He looked as if he had planned to say much more, but he'd run out of energy, or breath, after one sentence.

"Boys will protect," Papa said in a clear statement of fact, "don't fight that." Papa took one more slow breath and finished, "Promise me that."

"Yes, Papa." Angelina realized that these statements were never questions and were not meant to be challenged.

"My love, my life, my Angel," he said with more clarity and more volume than anything he'd said in months.

Angelina sat up straight, as Papa's renewed strength seemed to suggest more was coming.

"Tell Bobby," was all that followed, however. With that, Papa slowly turned his face back to the window, signaling that today's discussion was now over.

Angelina didn't struggle with Papa's message. His one- or two-word statements were always quite clear to family members. Her job was to tell Bobby everything she knew, and could remember, about her attacker in Oyster Park. Angelina had no doubt how it would end up after she informed Bobby, but she was certainly not going to disobey Papa again.

Not again.

DAY 14

Thursday. 9:45 am -- LA County Jail

Hector awoke as the large policeman was opening his cell. Over the course of Hector's four days in the LA County Central Jail, he had experienced numerous cellmates. However, for the past twelve hours or so, he'd been alone in his cell.

"Alvarez, Hector," the cop barked as he opened the sliding door, "on your feet and face your bunk."

As Hector stood up from the lower of the two bunk beds on which he'd been sleeping, the police officer grabbed Hector's shoulders and turned him facing the beds. With his back to the cop, he felt the officer grab his left wrist and pull it behind his back. Then he heard the familiar sound of the officer removing his handcuffs from his belt and securing Hector's left wrist.

The pain shot right up Hector's arm as the skinny metal cuff was tightened down over his bruised and tender wrist. After securing the right wrist with the second cuff, the officer led Hector out of the cell and down a long, narrow hallway. When they got to a series of six doors, each with a small viewing window, the officer stopped and tapped on the second one on the right.

Another police officer, from inside the room, opened the door and grabbed Hector's arm at the bicep. "Sit at the table -- feet on the floor, back against the chair." He sounded like he'd said that line a thousand times before, and emotionally he sounded no more interested than Hector felt.

The room was tiny. Just big enough to hold a small square table with four wooden chairs. The cinder-block walls were neither painted nor decorated. Sitting at the table was a young, white, nervous-looking man in a cheap suit. He had his suit coat hung on the back of his chair, exposing his white dress shirt and light blue tie. His shirt had clearly been through many meetings like this before, as it had noticeable yellow stains around the brim of the collar and under the arms.

"Please," the man at the table said, pointing to the chair directly across the table from him.

Hector sat, and the police officer shut the door but remained on the inside of the room. He stood straight and tall, with his eyes fixed across the room, as if to suggest he had virtually no interest in the meeting taking place at the table.

"My name is Darrin Tressel, and I'm a public defender for Los Angeles County." As he spoke, he seemed to enunciate each word perfectly, while placing extra emphasis on every other word. Hector instantly thought he sounded like every teacher he'd ever hated in school. It was a sound that suggested superiority, or that his audience couldn't keep up with his intellect unless he gave extra attention to every word.

"I understand that you declined your own legal representation," Mr. Tressel said, in more of a question than a statement. When Hector gave no response, Tressel added, "Is that true?"

"I don't have a lawyer," Hector said with virtually no emotion. "Is that your question?"

"Yes, I'm a court-appointed attorney, and I'll be representing you on this case."

"I know the drill," Hector admitted. It certainly wasn't his first experience with the legal system of LA County.

"May I call you Hector?" Tressel asked.

"May I call you Darrin?" Hector countered, to quickly make sure that his attorney didn't try to play any superiority cards on him.

"Sure," Tressel replied. "Hector, do you have any family members or friends that you need me to contact on your behalf?"

Hector just shook his head no and looked to the floor.

"Hector, I've read the police crime report regarding the activities at Oyster Regional Park on Friday night. I think it would be wise if you read it too. It's important that you and I discuss the events of Friday night and determine where there are differences versus the crime report."

Darrin Tressel reached to his right and revealed a black leather briefcase. It looked more like the kind that would hold a computer and not much else. As he unzipped the case, it was clear that it did not contain a laptop but rather was filled with manila folders and pads of yellow legal paper. Tressel retrieved a manila folder with a red tab that read "Alvarez, Hector – RL46809." He withdrew a memo that appeared to be seven or eight pages of small type.

Tressel slid the document across the table to Hector.

Hector read the title on the memo:

> Crime Report -- Pico Rivera Officer, Dennis Patrick
>
> Date: February 24
>
> Location: Oyster Regional Park
>
> Time: Between 10:10–10:45 pm

As he began to read the small print that described the activities, Hector realized that it would take him forever to read the entire document -- not to mention the numerous words that he didn't understand.

"Don't need to read that," Hector said, looking up at Tressel.

"Why not?" Tressel asked curiously.

"Look, I grabbed her. I hooked her to that metal bar in the park," Hector said, void of any emotion and with his eyes directly focused on Tressel's eyes. "I would have nailed her till she couldn't walk," Hector confirmed, "but super-cop showed up out of nowhere and saved her precious little ass."

Hector leaned back against his bound arms and looked at the ceiling. His head started to pound as he thought about the body slam he'd received from the officer in the park.

"Hector, did you touch her" -- Tressel's words were very slow and clearly enunciated -- "sexually, in any way?"

Hector reconnected with Tressel's eyes. "Didn't have the chance," he admitted. "Rambo shows up with a spotlight and spoiled the moment." As Hector finished his statement, he turned his head to the cop posted at the door to see if his comments had created any noticeable reaction.

They had not.

"You stunned her with the Taser?" Tressel asked slowly.

"Yep."

"You tied her to the playground apparatus?"

"Yep."

"Why was she naked?" Tressel questioned.

"I cut off her clothes," Hector said matter-of-factly. "Bitch wasn't even wearing a bra."

"Hector, did you write on her back with lipstick?"

"Yep."

"Why did you do that?"

"Needed to set the record straight, that's all," Hector said, leaving Tressel more confused than ever.

"I don't understand," Tressel admitted.

"That's because the note on her back wasn't for you," Hector said.

"Who was it for?" Tressel said quickly, losing the perfect pronunciation for the first time in their meeting.

"That's none of your business," Hector said as he stood to signify that their first meeting was officially over.

"Let me be as clear as I can with you, Hector," Tressel said, exaggerating each syllable as he spoke. "If your intention was to scare this girl -- that is one charge. If your intention was to rape her, that is quite another charge, and sentence. I hope, for your sake, that your real intention was to terrify this girl and make her think you were going to sexually abuse her, but your only real intention was to leave that message on her back. In fact, you were able to finish your message, and you had no intention of any actions beyond that -- other than to scare her a bit."

Hector remained silent, as he wasn't exactly sure what his new lawyer was trying to convey.

Tressel began to gather his papers into his briefcase and said, "I'd rather not hear any more from you on that topic. I believe your reason for being in that park was simply to scare this girl and leave a message on her back. While this is certainly a crime -- and one you'll need to serve time for -- it is entirely different than attempted rape." With that, Tressel stood and motioned to the guard at the door and repeated, "If that is what happened that night, it would be the best outcome for you, Hector."

DAY 15

Friday, 2:10 pm -- Los Angeles District Attorney's Office

"Snapshot, please," LA District Attorney Geoff Robbins said to his star pupil as they reached the part of their agenda that read State of California v. Hector Alvarez.

"This one is about as neatly wrapped as we get," Matula began, suggesting that the case required very little incremental work on behalf of the DA's office.

"Go," Robbins shot back, always encouraging Chris to say more, with fewer words.

"Cop pulls into Oyster Park with lights off; hears an electrical zap-like sound coming from the kids' play area; hits the area with his floodlight to surprise our defendant, Mr. Hector Alvarez, with his dick literally in his hand." Chris had been waiting to use that analogy ever since he first read about the case and later talked to Officer Patrick.

With no visual reaction from Robbins thus far, Chris continued.

"Alvarez has his pants around his ankles and a Taser gun in his hand. He is standing inches away from a completely naked and completely unconscious Angelina Carbona Constanzio." Chris liked to use the victim's full name to create the verbal effect of thoroughness of his summary.

"Cop chases, tackles, and arrests Alvarez; Constanzio is bound to a metal tic-tac-toe game in the playground, feet pulled apart, hands bound behind her back." Matula took a small pause to allow Robbins to chime in, but Geoff still hand no visible reaction.

"She'd been hit twice with a Taser, according to the doctors at Mission, but had no signs of sexual penetration. She had nearly an inch of duct

107

tape wrapped around her mouth." Matula took a breath and glanced back at his notes, to let Robbins soak in the information he had provided thus far.

"That it?" Robbins asked.

"The only other marking on the victim, besides the bruising from the zip ties he used to bind her and the facial abrasions from both the duct tape and banging the metal structure, was a message left in red lipstick on her back." Matula paused to wait for that the sink in and to wait for Robbins to ask for more.

"A lipstick message on her back?"

"Yep," Matula built to his big finish, "the message said NO LIMITS, and the suspect had the lipstick container tucked in his sock. That, in addition to a Berretta nine-millimeter, some broken zip ties, and a nasty-looking serrated-edge hunting knife."

Matula sat back, pretty proud of his two-minute recap.

"So," Robbins said, dragging out the word as if he was still thinking about what to say next, "he did not rape her?"

"Evidently never penetrated," Matula responded.

"So we can go for kidnapping, assault, and attempted rape, but likely no more than that," Robbins concluded in a half statement, half question.

"Isn't that enough?" Matula said, trying to figure out why his boss wasn't congratulating him for a quick and thorough summary.

"Not to get Alvarez off the street forever, no," Robbins stated.

"Is this another one of those regulars, whom you plea out because the difference between plea and trial sentence is insignificant?" Matula was immediately frustrated that this topic was surfacing again.

"Maybe," Robbins said. "Probably," he added as he thought some more.

DAY 15
Friday, 6:55 pm -- Outback Steakhouse

Frank was glad the traffic was light and that he'd gotten to Outback a full half hour before he had agreed to meet Bobby. He knew Bobby would be on time for their 7:30 dinner -- Bobby was always on time, and usually early.

Frank walked through the front door and headed to the bar, figuring he'd get a drink or two before securing a table for their meeting.

"Hey, Uncle Frank." Frank was visibly startled by the unexpected yell, but he certainly recognized Bobby's voice before he saw his face.

Sitting at the far end of the bar, Bobby was nursing a draft beer.

"You're early," Frank said, giving Bobby the customary bear hug.

"Ditto," Bobby replied.

"Traffic was light," Frank started, "and to be honest, I was ready to talk. Sitting around doing nothing was eating me up inside." Bobby nodded his head, agreeing with Frank's comments.

"Agreed," Bobby concurred with as few words as possible. "Angelina is doing better, and I'm convinced she'll be fine, with a little time," Bobby said in a pretty convincing tone. "Between you and I, Uncle Frank, and only between you and I," Bobby was confirming that neither would include Papa in his next statement, "this might turn out to be exactly what Ang needed."

"How do you figure that?" Frank said in his usual slow and steady dialogue.

"Ang got a hell of a scare, but luckily she wasn't really hurt, at least not physically," Bobby said. "She hates the way we watch her, but now I think she understands the importance of our safety net."

After thinking about his own words for a second, Bobby added, "And I think she'll take a few more precautions going forward."

"Tough way to learn that lesson, but you're probably right. It could have been much, much worse," Frank agreed.

"So, what's next?" Frank cut right to the heart of their meeting, because he knew that was why Bobby wanted to meet, and he knew that patience was not Bobby's strength.

"We end the Alvarez-Constanzio thing right now," Bobby said with a tone of a head coach, giving a pregame speech. "I don't want to worry about that little shit ever again, and I don't want Ang lookin' over her shoulder, wondering if he's there."

"Where is Hector now?" Frank asked, with complete confidence that Bobby knew the answer.

"Locked up, downtown. He's awaiting the preliminary hearing," he responded without hesitation. "If he goes straight to prison, we're kind of shit out of luck," Bobby continued. "It's likely he'll go away for five to ten years, so we'll simply have to keep an eye on his release."

"Bobby, isn't there a way to get to Alvarez, even if he's in prison," Frank said, admittedly way out of his comfort zone of knowledge.

"Uncle Frank, you've been watching too many episode of The Sopranos," Bobby chuckled. "It ain't easy to get to someone on the inside."

Even as Bobby said it aloud, his mind was racing on how he might be able to execute an in-prison retaliation. He knew it was unlikely, but he also knew that Papa wouldn't take "unlikely" as an answer.

"Understood," Frank said in response.

Bobby leaned forward and said, "Listen, I think you and I need to go sit with Papa. He'll have some advice on what to do next. Either way, he needs to know what's happening with Alvarez."

"Pick a day and a time, and I'll meet you at Mission," Frank said referring to Papa's hospital residence for the past one hundred days or so.

DAY 18
Monday, 11:15 am -- Los Angeles District Attorney's Office

Chris Matula had taken over the smaller of the two conference rooms in the DA's offices. It was a habit that hadn't won him any friends among his peers, because he'd lay all his evidence out in sequential order, with Post-it notes and a strategically placed easel or two -- so the conference room was completely unusable to anyone else when Matula was preparing a case.

A few of the other assistant DAs had complained to their boss about Matula's little land grab, but the truth was that Geoff Robbins kind of liked the approach. It ensured that Matula's cases were logical and understandable for a judge or jury and quickly identified missing pieces of a puzzle. Robbins knew it was a bit unfair to the others, but since the distribution of caseload was also unfair, with Matula consistently getting the more difficult and higher-profile cases, he figured he'd leave it alone.

Chris stepped back from the cluttered conference table and mentally reviewed the facts. He had called his assistant, Julie, to be his audience and his sounding board. Julie was very familiar with this process. She rarely said a word during one of Chris' verbal outlines, because he really wasn't talking to her or asking for feedback. She was convinced that he really just wanted to hear his own voice and didn't want to look weird talking to himself in the conference room.

"Okay, here's the lay of the land, so far," he began, looking more at the adjacent wall than at Julie, who was sitting at the far end of the long, narrow table.

"February 6, Hector's brother is beaten to death and dumped in a dumpster."

112

Julie cringed at the thought, but her slight gasp didn't distract Chris at all.

"February 9, witnesses say that Angelina Constanzio was seen at the cemetery gathering for Juan's funeral. She didn't appear to talk to anyone and apparently came alone. That Friday afternoon, February 13, Angelina loses her cell phone while hanging out with her friends."

Matula took a quick look at Julie, to make sure she was following the flow. Her verbal head nod told him to keep going.

"That night, Angelina's friends get text messages from her phone that they think are from her, confirming her plans to join them at Oyster Regional Park."

Holding up a picture of Angelina's cell phone, Matula continued, "Meanwhile, Angelina's best friend receives a text from Angelina's phone, from someone who claimed to have found the phone and would meet them at Oyster Park to return it."

"Hector had her phone?" Julie asked, trying to jump to an obvious conclusion, based on what she'd heard so far.

"They found Angelina's phone on the large rocket structure at Oyster's playground area, and her friends confirm that she didn't have it when she arrived at the park -- so I think it's safe to say Hector had it," Matula said with a hint of sarcasm.

"We're trying to pull prints from the phone, but usually those little stainless steel models have so many smudge marks overlapping that you never get a clean print," Chris explained.

"Angelina's friends walk into the park to meet up with the others, while she goes toward the street to meet the mysterious phone returner."

"Nice friends -- letting her go alone." Julie couldn't help herself.

"Yeah, none of them had a good answer for that," he agreed, "but somehow Hector got her separated from the pack. Based on the materials found in the rocket ship, as well as Angelina's phone, it seems logical that Hector was hiding in there." Matula leafed through a pile of pictures and finally found the close-up of the park's rocket ship structure.

"She would have walked straight through the play area to get to the street, based on where her friends parked," Chris said while using a pointer to suggest her path via an aerial map of Oyster Park that was taped to an easel pad next to the conference table.

"Given the two contact burns on Angelina's neck and shoulder, he must have hit her twice with the Taser gun as she passed him in the play area."

Julie chose not to look at the pictures of Angelina's neck and shoulder marks. The fact was that rape was not an easy topic for her to listen to, and Angelina was closer to her age than she cared to admit. Julie knew that Chris would never understand her personal reaction to this topic, so she simply closed her eyes, to ensure that Chris wouldn't hand her any more pictures.

"Hector than used zip ties to bind Angelina's wrists behind her back and bind her ankles to this tic-tac-toe wall," Chris said as he quickly searched the materials on the table, looking for the picture of the playground apparatus. "He bent her, face first, over this metal structure, and cut all her clothes off with a hunting knife."

Julie had reopened her eyes but was trying to not form the mental picture that Chris was slowly describing. Young, single females in a large city like LA learned to handle a lot of things on their own -- but the truth was, they always had a healthy fear of rape.

"Hector then takes lipstick and writes the words No Limits on her back." Chris used his fingers to suggest quotes around the words, but the picture of Angelina's naked back with the smudged words made it painfully clear.

"Hard to know what he meant by that, but the police found the same lipstick container in Hector's sock when they arrested him."

Chris paused, to check his own story. He liked the flow and believed he could paint a vivid picture, given the maps of Oyster Regional Park, the actual tic-tac-toe structure, and the photographs of Angelina's wounds.

"I might have the small tic-tac-toe structure removed from the play area and brought to the trial courtroom," Chris said as he envisioned a very graphic and compelling courtroom scene. "I can use a mannequin and bind its legs to the structure and bend it over the metal wall— showing how her back would be exposed for this lipstick message."

Chris' face couldn't hold back a jubilant smile as he considered this tactic. Julie was visibly shaken and started to squirm a bit in her seat as he described the potential courtroom prop.

"Chris, I think I'd better get back to work," Julie lied, in an effort to escape any further descriptions of the scene.

"Okay, Julie." Chris could see that his recap had bothered her to the point of her seeking escape. He smiled again as he was imagining how six or seven female jurors would squirm as he slowly narrated the events of Oyster Park.

He knew he had a good one. In law school, he had a professor who always said, "Certain cases bring out the natural talents of certain lawyers." Chris was certain that The State of California v. Hector Alvarez would bring out his natural talents.

He figured Robbins would push for a quick plea, and Hector's lawyer would have no choice but to seek a plea. The only thing Chris was missing was a good reason not to plea this case. One thing was certain; this case could make Chris' career, and as such, he had to avoid a plea bargain.

DAY 19
Tuesday, 10:20 am -- Mission Hospital

When Frank entered Papa's hospital room, Bobby was already there. Even though Bobby had agreed to meet him there at 10:30 am, Frank was certainly not surprised to see Bobby already having a discussion with Papa.

Probably got here over an hour ago, Frank thought to himself as he entered the room with a slight knock on the door.

"What's up, Uncle Frank," Bobby said, to announce Frank's arrival to his father and to immediately end any conversation that Papa and Bobby were having.

"Papa, Bobby, good morning," Frank said in his usual slow and steady way.

"What's new to report, Frank?" Papa said as he turned toward Frank and raised his hand, leaving his elbow and upper arm on the hospital mattress.

Frank stepped forward and squeezed Papa's slightly raised hand. "No news yet on a prelim date, but I assume they'll be doing the arraignment this week."

Frank knew that both Papa and Bobby understood the legal process better than most lawyers. Hector would need to go to an arraignment first, where the charges would be brought against him, and Hector would likely plea not guilty. From there, the judge would set a high bail for Hector and establish a date for the preliminary hearing, where the District Attorney's office would have to share its evidence and witness list, to prove that there was adequate proof to proceed to a jury trial. The likelihood was that this case would never even make

116

it beyond a preliminary hearing, as Hector would be forced to find a settlement plea, given the overwhelming evidence against him.

"In fact, from what I understand, the paperwork for the arraignment is filed, and a judge named Henderson will be handling the case," Bobby chimed in, to add to Frank's comment.

"I'm guessing both the arraignment and the prelim will be quick," Frank continued. "Alvarez has a court-appointed attorney," Frank said, checking his small spiral notebook for assistance, "young guy named Tressel. Pretty sure he's got nothing to work with. I'd expect he'll try to work a plea with the DA, maybe even before the prelim."

"Papa, what's your best guess on a plea for the little shit?" Bobby asked, knowing that Papa's perspective was as qualified as any judge's. When it came to knowing the legal system and probable outcomes, Papa was certainly qualified to answer the question.

"Probably go for kidnapping," Papa said, conserving his breath between each word, "which should plea out to about nine years."

"How about the rape?" Bobby shot back.

"Only attempted rape, B." Papa used Bobby's childhood nickname, his first initial, more to conserve words than for any other reason. "That will only plea out to about seven or eight."

Both visitors remained silent to see if Papa had finished speaking.

"Combined, I'd be surprised," Papa said, clearly calculating in his head, "to see it be more that eleven or twelve years in a final plea."

"Which means the little sack of shit only serves six or seven years, right?" Bobby said with clear disgust.

"Less," Papa said, returning to his one word answers.

"How much less?" Bobby asked.

"Less," Papa repeated.

"Papa, will Hector get out while he awaits trial?" Frank asked, reminding Bobby there could be a window of time when Hector would be on the streets.

"Big bail," Papa said.

"Could we," Bobby said, obviously still forming his thoughts as he spoke, "anonymously post bail for Mr. Alvarez?" Bobby smiled as he said it. No matter how Papa answered, Bobby was proud of himself for thinking around the obstacles.

"Interesting," Papa said, staring straight at Bobby. "Probably not, but I like your thinking, son."

They all stayed quiet, to give Papa time to think.

"At prelim," Papa started, "I want every male family member present. Not Ang, and none of her friends -- but every member of our family. Understood?"

Frank and Bobby looked at each other, but Papa wanted a verbal response.

"Understood?" Papa said in a voice louder than either Bobby or Frank had heard come from Papa in nearly four months.

"Absolutely," Bobby said.

"Yes," Frank added.

"I want Alvarez to see the enemy," Papa said without sounding winded or stopping for more breath, "the minute he steps out of the jail and into that courtroom."

DAY 20
<u>Wednesday, 11:40 am -- Los Angeles</u>
<u>District Attorney Office</u>

"Gotta minute, chief?" Chris Matula usually stopped by his boss' office in person, but today he made a call from his conference room bunker.

"What do you need?" was DA Robbins' response, clearly suggesting that this was not a great time to ask.

"I want to walk you through the Alvarez case," Matula responded. "As I'm sure you've heard, I've commandeered the little conference room again."

"Listen, I don't have time to be your mock jury, Chris; that's what paralegals are for." Robbins knew that if he went down to the conference room, his whole afternoon would be shot.

"This thing can really be powerful in court. The overwhelming evidence, the brutality of his approach -- I think we can get a jury to think rape, even though he was arrested before he got started."

Robbins could hear the excitement and eagerness in his young protégé's voice. "Chris, this thing will plea out before you leave court at the arraignment."

"Geoff, you told me once that this job will challenge you to soften your principles. Do you remember saying that?"

"I plead the fifth," Robbins said slowly, afraid of where his star pupil might be taking this conversation.

"You said, and I quote, 'Have the balls to stand your ground when you're sure you're right.' I think this is one of those times." Matula let

119

that hang in the air for a minute before he hit his boss with his final comment.

"I won't plea this. Alvarez got caught with a Taser gun in one hand and his johnson in the other. He had a seventeen-year-old girl strapped to a metal pole, and he was about to ruin her life. If that cop hadn't stumbled onto the scene, he would have hurt her badly." Matula could feel his face getting red and his mouth working hard to keep up with his mind. "This kid deserves every month, of every year, I can get him. I won't plea this one. You can fire me, pull me from the case, or back me on this one -- those are your options, chief."

DAY 21

Thursday, 2:50 pm -- Detective Felix Bernard's Office, LAPD

"Chris, this one is a little more complex than just some kid trying to nail a high school hottie on a Friday night," Detective Felix Bernard said while sitting in his office with his junior detective, Campbell Warner, and LA Assistant District Attorney Chris Matula.

Campbell knew that Detective Bernard didn't say things like "nail a high school hottie" very often, at least not in front of her. She was convinced that he was simply trying to make a point to the DA's office, that this crime was more than just a sex-crazed kid trying to score with some girl.

"No offense, Felix, but this one is as cut-and-dried as they come," Matula responded. "Caught the kid red-handed," he said as he smiled at Campbell, "no pun intended. He was carrying her lost cell phone, as well as a Taser, nine-millimeter pistol, hunting knife, and lipstick."

Matula turned his attention back to Bernard. "Let's not over-think this thing."

"Chris, I won't over-think it, as long as you don't under-think it," Bernard replied.

"I don't follow."

"Listen, about a week before Hector Alvarez straps young Angelina Constanzio to a park toy, his brother is beaten to death and tossed into a dumpster." Felix took a sip of Diet Coke and nodded to Campbell, as if to say "jump in if you have anything to add."

Campbell took the hint and continued where Bernard had left off. "There are no legitimate leads on Juan Alvarez's murder, but it's hard to believe there is no connection between Hector's actions and his brother's demise."

"Any connections to Angelina or the Constanzio family?" Matula asked.

"None that we've found," Campbell quickly responded. "We did see a lipstick message in an apartment that Hector shared with his brother." Campbell continued her stare at Matula and reiterated her point, "Yes, a lipstick message -- written on his glass patio door. It was just one word, the name Angelina," she said, using her fingers to suggest quotes as she said Angelina's name. "It looked to us like there may have been more to the message, but the rest of the window had recently been cleaned."

"Maybe Hector wrote her name," Matula said nonchalantly. "In fact, that makes perfect sense that he had a thing for her and wrote his target's name in lipstick."

Detective Felix chimed back in, "Maybe, but if your brother had just been killed and you just buried him, do you shift your attention to some girl you've got the hots for?"

"Perhaps," Matula quickly shot back. "Who knows how a pissed-off nineteen-year-old reacts to losing a family member."

"Pissed off, we agree on," Bernard answered. "Hector would have been frustrated and pissed off," he said, turning his focus to his partner. "What we can't figure out is why that anger would be focused on Angelina Constanzio."

"Does it really matter why?" Matula said, in an effort to end the conversation and return his focus to all the evidence against Hector.

"It matters if Hector's lawyer can show that Hector's actions were somehow in revenge for Juan's death. It may not mean much to you, legally," Bernard said, taking another quick sip of cola, "but you and I both know it would make a shitload of difference to twelve jurors."

Matula sat quietly for a second, internalizing what Bernard had said. He hated the fact that Bernard was right.

"Unfortunately, the only one that can connect the dots on Juan and Angelina Constanzio is Hector," Campbell said, putting the final touches on their meeting. "We'll keep pushing for more facts, Mr. Matula, but be aware that there may be more to this attempted rape than we thought."

DAY 22

Friday, 8:30 am -- LA County Jail

"Alvarez, Hector -- on your feet."

Hector heard the voice well before the police guard appeared at his cell. "Alvarez, I said on your feet," said the muscle-bound twenty-something officer as he unlocked Hector's jail cell and slid open the door. "You've got a visitor."

"Who is it?" Hector said groggily, as he swung his legs off the bed and rubbed the sleep from his eyes.

"I ain't your doorman, Alvarez," the guard barked. "Just get on your feet and put your hands behind your back."

Hector did as instructed, and "steroid boy," as Hector had silently called this particular guard for the past few days, applied cuffs to Hector's still-swollen wrists. The guard led Hector back to the same set of doors he'd been to once before and deposited him in the same room where he'd met Darrin Tressel just a week earlier.

The guards followed the same procedure -- steroid boy knocked on the door, causing the guard on the inside to open the door. Once Hector was in the room, the internal guard closed the door and remained inside.

Hector recognized his lawyer, seated at the same table in the same chair as their last visit. While Tressel's suit and tie were a different color, he appeared to be wearing the same discolored white shirt from last week.

He looks like he's had a tougher week than I've had, Hector said to himself as he took a seat at the table.

"Hello again, Hector," Tressel started.

"'Sup," Hector mumbled in response.

"Listen, Hector," Tressel said, sitting back in his chair in a relaxing pose, "I've read the full crime report, I've met with the arresting officer, and I've reviewed the evidence of the case." Tressel folded his arms as if he was quite pleased with the effort he'd applied thus far to Hector's case. However, it was clear by Hector's emotionless, reactionless body language that his client did not concur.

"I think it's time you and I had an honest discussion about your options."

While Hector could care less about the opinion of Darrin Tressel, he figured his time in this little meeting room was better than lying on his bunk staring at the bunk above him, so he figured he'd play along and hear what his attorney had to say.

"Say what you came to say," Hector said reluctantly.

"Here's the deal," Tressel began as he retrieved a legal-sized pad of yellow paper from his briefcase. Hector could see that the pad was already full of Tressel's notes. "Based on the Taser gun in your hand, soon to be confirmed by fingerprints, and the Taser marks on the victim's shoulder and neck, they've got you on assault."

Tressel paused to give Hector time to react or refute what he'd heard. Unfortunately for Tressel, his client remained motionless.

"They'll likely go for kidnapping, since she was bound to the playground against her will. She was bound against her will, right, Hector?"

Hector thought of a couple of smartass comments, but he didn't want to piss off his lawyer so bad that he'd cut the meeting short, so he kept his answers short and sweet.

"Yeah, I tased her, then I tied her up."

Tressel jotted down a quick note on his already-full scribble pad and continued. "Since the only witnesses were you, the victim, and the arresting officer, neither side has a lot to decipher. She was unconscious when the cop arrived, and you were holding a Taser gun and zip tie."

Hector had no reaction, but continued to maintain his eye contact with Tressel.

"That leaves the charge of rape. Hector, if you never touched that girl, sexually, they'll be forced to stay with attempted rape." Tressel let that statement hang in the air, as both a question and a statement.

After a few seconds of silence, Tressel asked, "Hector, I need you to think this all the way through. Did you touch that girl, in any way, sexually?" Tressel put obvious emphasis on the word any, as he needed to know if his client had done more than the arresting officer or the victim's doctors had concluded.

"Nope." Hector didn't need time; the question was simple, and his answer was too.

"Nothing with your fingers or with any object whatsoever? No rubbing, petting, or protruding of any kind?" he asked, again with a verbal emphasis on any kind.

"Nothing," Hector said flatly.

Tressel sat back and stared at his client for what seemed like a full minute, as if evaluating the truthfulness of his statement. Hector thought the prolonged silence was some sort of trick or legal strategy to get him to blurt out more facts. When Hector remained still, Tressel finally broke the silence.

"In that case, they have to stay with attempted rape. Even better, all they have is you with your pants down. They can't prove what you were planning on doing. Like I said before, if your real objective was simply to leave a note on her back and give her a good scare, they'll struggle to convict on attempted rape. Do you understand that, Hector?"

Tressel again sat back and crossed his arms, like he had just won something. It was clear that Darrin Tressel was pleased with small mental victories.

"Just so we're clear," Hector said, staring at his court-appointed attorney, "if RoboCop hadn't showed up in the nick of time, I'd have ..."

"Whoa, whoa, that's enough," Tressel interrupted loudly. "I prefer you keep any thoughts on what might have happened to yourself! Let's keep our dialogue based only on what actually did happen at that park!"

"Listen, you can do whatever legal game you want to do. I don't give a shit, either way," Hector continued, "but that little cunt got lucky, and she knows it."

Tressel sat straight up in his chair and put his elbows on the rickety table that separated the two. He took a quick look at the police guard at the door, who continued to stare straight ahead, and then looked to his client.

"Hector, listen to me. With rape of a seventeen-year-old, you go away, and maybe never come back," Tressel said, trying to jolt his new client into some kind of reaction. "With attempted rape of a seventeen-year-old girl, you might get the same thing. But with assault and kidnapping only, you'll spend some serious time in prison, but you'll get out at a pretty young age, and you'll still have the majority of your life to live."

Tressel was now leaning forward, locked on to Hector's eyes. "Do you understand what I'm saying, Hector? Assault, kidnapping, and a lewd sexual act is a tough jail sentence, no doubt; but if you tell anyone, including me, that you were going to rape that girl, you're not getting out of prison until you are a very old man."

Tressel sat back, and as he did, he reiterated his last point one more time for his client, "Anyone!"

Hector finally moved, sitting straight up in his chair. "Dude, prison don't bother me, okay," he said in an effort to take control of the discussion. "In fact, prison sounds pretty good to me, if you want to know the real fuckin' truth. I ain't got nothing on the outside waitin' for me. You guys in the business suits aren't giving real work to any spick with a prison record, so what do you think I'll do for money on the outside?"

Hector saw that his lawyer was a bit startled by his comments and clearly speechless for the first time since they'd met.

"I don't want any special shit worked out between lawyers. Is that clear? I think whatever a jury of my peers decides," Hector said, pointing at himself with his bound hands and stressing the words my peers, "will be okay by me."

Hector relaxed back into his chair, having said his piece, and waited for Tressel's response.

"Are you saying you don't want me to get you a plea bargain?" Tressel asked in disbelief. "Listen, Hector, I'll get you the best possible outcome, and I'll do that by negotiating with the District Attorney's office." Tressel's voice was no longer slow and punctuated, but somewhat desperate and pleading.

"We don't want this thing to go to trial; that much I can assure you," Tressel continued. "A jury will, no doubt, look at that high school girl tied to a playground fixture and choose to send you away for as long as they possibly can." Tressel stared right at his client and added, "Trust me, a jury trial is not in your best interest."

Hector looked away. He was done listening to Darrin Tressel. "This jail here is better than prison." He continued to stare blankly at the cinder-block wall. "I get to stay here while we're in court, right? I want a trial, hopefully a nice long one. I'll only say what you want me to say and nothing more." Hector returned his gaze to his attorney and added, "But I have the right to a trial, and I know a trial will take a long fuckin' time." Hector paused and thought for a second and said, "I got time, and I don't care how long I go to prison."

"Hector, I think you ...," Tressel started to say, but was immediately interrupted by his client.

"No deals, Mr. Lawyer," Hector shouted loudly, to stop Tressel's response. "No deals and a long trial. That's it."

With that, Hector stood up and nodded to the officer guarding the door, as if to say "time's up."

"Okay, Hector," Tressel said quickly, to stop his exit. "So let's talk about the arraignment."

Hector stopped and looked back over his shoulder.

"The legal system has three clear steps to trial," Tressel began, returning to a slow, measured pace. "First, is the arraignment, where the prosecutor officially charges you with a crime and you enter a plea -- usually guilty, or not guilty." Tressel had flipped his legal pad over to the brown cardboard backing and was using it to draw a three-circle diagram.

"An arraignment simply is there to see if you plead guilty, in which case it's game over, and the judge can sentence you. If you plead not guilty, the judge will set bail and then set a date for your preliminary hearing." Tressel pointed to his second circle, which he'd drawn just beneath the first one. "At your preliminary hearing, the prosecutor is required to prove that he has enough evidence to warrant a full trial. If the judge agrees, then he sets an actual court date, including jury selection, etcetera."

Moving his pen to the third circle, Tressel continued, "That takes you to a trial, where twelve jurors will hear testimony from witnesses, review the physical evidence, and eventually render a decision on each charge that was brought against you."

Tressel looked up from his pad to see if his client was following his Judicial System 101 overview. "Does that make sense?"

"Thanks for the legal recap, Darrin," Hector said sarcastically, "but that's for you to know, not me."

"Throughout this process, which will likely take about six months or so just to get to trial," Tressel said, "the judge will be pushing both sides, me and the DA, to come to an agreement, in order to avoid a full trial."

"But if I want a trial, can I get one anyway?"

"Everyone has the right to a trial, if that's their preference," Tressel admitted reluctantly.

"That's what I want," Hector responded.

"We'll keep talking about that, you and I, as we go," Tressel said, saving this argument for another day, "but to get to a prelim, which leads to a trial, it all starts with an arraignment. It's simple stuff -- the judge reads the charges brought against you, and you say, 'Not guilty, your honor.' From there, he sets a preliminary date."

"What if I am guilty?" Hector questioned honestly.

"If you say guilty, there is no trial, no prelim, and no more staying in this jail. The judge will sentence you, either right there or a few days later, and you go straight to prison."

"So, if I want to go through all three circles," Hector said, pointing to the diagram that Tressel had made on the back of his legal pad, "then I need to say 'not guilty'?"

"Let's say, 'not guilty, your honor.' Can't hurt to show the judge a little respect," Tressel replied.

"Okay, 'not guilty, your honor,'" Hector repeated with a little chuckle.

"Then he'll set a bail, set a prelim date, and that will give us time to talk more about getting a better deal," Tressel said.

Hector turned back to the guard and nodded again. This time the guard opened the door and grabbed Hector's arm to lead him back to his cell. Hector looked back as he exited and said, "No deals, Mr. Lawyer. I'll say 'not guilty' when you tell me to, but I'm going to have a trial."

DAY 22

Friday, 9:35 am -- Los Angeles Superior Court

"What's up, Kobe?" Helen said as her boss arrived and headed toward her desk on the way to his chambers.

"Lakers call with a contract yet?" he joked in return.

"Yes, they did, in fact," Helen played along. "They said if you want to retain your season tickets for future seasons, you'll need to start giving more games to your kick-ass senior clerk."

"They said that, huh?"

"Almost verbatim, sir." Helen handed Judge Henderson two green, legal-sized hanging folders and one pink voice mail slip as he reached her desk.

"Arraignment briefs on both the Alvarez and Warner cases," she said, tapping her index finger on the green files, "both requesting prelims with you ASAP."

"Anything else?" the judge asked, pausing for a second at her desk before proceeding to his office. "Anything other than the call from the Lakers and two arraignment briefs?"

"Yes, you got a call from DA Robbins this morning. He requested a fifteen-minute chat, either by phone or in person. He said that was your call."

"Did he say what it was in reference to?"

"Nope. I asked if he'd like me to include a subject on the note, but he said he'd rather wait until you talked," Helen said, and then added, "Everything you need for today is on your desk."

As the judge reached his door, he was startled by Helen.

"Oh, Judge. I completely forgot, but your daughter called yesterday while you were at the Y."

Henderson froze to hear everything Helen had to say about the call with his youngest child and only daughter, Tonya.

"She called on your cell phone, which by the way, you never take with you."

"Afraid I'll lose it," Henderson admitted, still not turning around from the door to his chambers.

"That's exactly what I told Tonya." She laughed referring to his twenty-year-old college sophomore. "We both had a good laugh about how the term mobile doesn't apply to your phone. Your phone never travels, except from your desk to your briefcase."

"Did she have anything else to say?"

"I don't think so. Sounded like she just called to say hi to her dad and to see if his knees had finally given out."

"Remind me to call her after lunch. I don't think she even wakes up until 10:30 or so," he said. "Life is good at age twenty, huh, Helen?"

"I can't remember twenty, which means you definitely can't," she mused.

"Sad, but true," he said, finally opening his door to start his morning routine. "If the Lakers call, interrupt me," he said, disappearing into his office, "but other than that, give me a silent hour to read these briefs."

DAY 22

Friday, 5:50 pm -- Interstate 5 Southbound

Judge Henderson retrieved the phone message from the front pocket of his dress shirt. He had been meaning to call DA Geoff Robbins back all day, but a combination of unexpected legal briefs and a flood of calls had overwhelmed his afternoon.

He dialed the number for Robbins' cell phone, which Helen had written on the note, and waited for his Bluetooth feature to connect his call through the radio on his Lexus Land Cruiser.

Robbins picked up on the second ring, with noisy background chatter. "Robbins here," he said.

"Geoff, it's Judge Henderson, returning your call. Did I catch you at a bad time?" the judge said, noticing the noise in the background.

"Your honor," Robbins responded in a high-pitched surprised tone, "give me five quick seconds, please, to excuse myself from this meeting."

Judge Henderson was moving along the I-5 at normal Friday evening speeds, which meant less that ten miles per hour, so waiting was no problem. Henderson envisioned Robbins tossing all of his staff out to the hallway so that he could have a private conversation.

"Your honor, thanks for the call back."

"My pleasure," said Henderson. "Is the connection okay? I'm never sure how these Bluetooth calls sound, but wireless car conversations are now the law," he said chuckling.

"Connection is fine," Robbins answered. "The purpose for my call is a new case that you're set to arraign next week."

"If it's a new case, should we be talking about it?" the judge asked, knowing that he and the DA should not have private conversations about the specifics of any upcoming case.

"I'm not calling to discuss details of the case, or legal perspective," Robbins reassured him, "but rather to give you a heads-up about the DA's intention, as it relates to pleas."

"I don't follow you, Geoff," Henderson admitted.

"The case is assigned to Chris Matula, one of my assistant DAs. I think you know Chris?" he said, in the form of a question.

"We all know Half-Pipe." Henderson laughed, as he was certain that Robbins was aware of the nickname Matula had acquired among judges and clerks.

"Yes, well," Robbins said, giggling along with Henderson, "Half-Pipe is fired up on this particular case and is fighting any legal logic regarding plea bargains. The case is versus a nineteen-year-old male, Hector Alvarez, who is being charged with assault, kidnapping, and attempted rape."

"Let's not go any further with case specifics," Henderson appropriately warned. "I am familiar with the case and have the arraignment scheduled. So how can I help you, Geoff?"

"I wanted you to know that Chris is dead set against a plea, so if you find us being unreasonable in the plea process, that's the cause. I sort of give my guys a one-time pass to put their foot down; and this, evidently, is Matula's one time."

"Got it," Henderson said as he thought for a second. "Geoff, there may come a time in this case, as there is in any case, where the plea is better than a sentence you might get with a jury finding the defendant guilty."

"Your thinking is exactly the purpose for my call," Robbins admitted. "Should we reach that point in the Alvarez case, perhaps you and I can have an informal chat, and that logic may help my eager apprentice see the light."

"Understood, and agreed."

"May never be an issue," said Robbins, "but I thought it best to reach out in advance."

"No sweat. Thanks, Geoff." Henderson put the finishing touch on the call by adding, "For what it's worth, Geoff, Half-Pipe is a hell of a lawyer. We all poke fun at him because he's a little rough around the edges, but we're glad he's fighting for the state of California, and not for drug dealers."

"Couldn't agree more," Robbins concurred. "Have a nice weekend, your honor."

DAYS 26 - 32

PRELIMINARY HEARING ... PRELIMINARY JUSTICE

Hector was sitting on a long wooden bench with his hands cuffed in front of him, wearing a clean pair of orange pants and an orange short-sleeve shirt, compliments of the LA County Judicial System. He was seated alongside five other inmates, decked out in the same day-glow orange that he was wearing.

The six of them were located on the far side of the court, just behind a waist-high wooden wall that physically separated their bench from the courtroom. Hector assumed that there was a method for how they were aligned on the bench, as the guards were quite adamant about each inmate staying in his specific place. Once the courtroom process began, the logic of their order became clear -- they were aligned according to the order their cases would be addressed.

Hector was the third person on the bench, and based on the fact that his neighbor was now standing over at the defendant's table with a court-appointed lawyer, Hector figured he was next.

When his neighbor was escorted by the bailiff back to the wooden bench, Hector's heart started to beat a little faster.

"The court calls The State of California versus Hector Alvarez, case number RL46809," said a woman of no more than four feet tall, who appeared to be at least sixty years old. She was located just in front of the judge's huge raised desk. Next to the munchkin woman was a court reporter, who showed zero expression, as she typed at lightning speed on a little machine that looked like a shrunken cash register.

The bailiff tapped Hector on the arm and mumbled, "Come with me." As he led him to the defendant's table, Hector saw his lawyer for the first time. Darrin Tressel stood from his seat in the second row and came through the short swinging doors that separated the viewing seats from the actual courtroom.

"Remember, just keep standing, and say 'not guilty, your honor,' when you are asked," Tressel whispered to his client.

"I think I can handle that," Hector said sarcastically, and a little louder than Tressel would have liked. Hector had been watching the first two cases and knew just how mundane this process was for all the people involved.

"Assistant District Attorney Chris Matula for the state, your honor," the five-foot-high and three-foot-wide Matula said to the judge.

The judge appeared to be reading something, but given the height of his desk, Hector had no idea what it was.

"Darrin Tressel, court-appointed attorney for the defendant, Mr. Hector Alvarez, your honor," Tressel said confidently.

Judge Henderson opened a file, put on his cheater glasses, and read in silence for a few long seconds. Then he slowly looked up at Matula and said, "In the case of California versus Hector Alvarez, the state is charging Mr. Alvarez with assault with a deadly weapon, kidnapping of a minor, and attempted rape of a minor. Do I have that correct, Mr. Matula?"

"Yes, your honor."

Judge Henderson removed his glasses, set them on his desk, and turned his gaze to Hector and his lawyer.

"Mr. Alvarez, has your lawyer explained the arraignment process to your satisfaction?"

"Yes," was all Hector was comfortable saying in response.

"Very well. With regards to the charge of assault with a deadly weapon, how do you plea?" Henderson asked.

"Not guilty," Hector said shakily. He was trying to sound and look tough, but the entire courtroom setting had been a bad memory for him, and it simply rushed back difficult memories the minute he had entered.

"Your honor," Tressel whispered to his client without moving his lips, "don't forget to say 'your honor.'"

Judge Henderson continued with his questions, "With regards to the charge of kidnapping a minor, how do you plea, Mr. Alvarez?"

"Not guilty, your honor," Hector said, turning to his lawyer when he said it.

"With regards to the charge of attempted rape of a minor, how do you plea?"

"Not guilty, your honor," Hector said for the third time, and with noticeably more confidence than the first two.

"Very well," Judge Henderson concluded, putting his glasses back on the end of his nose but staring down at his desk. "Let the record reflect the charges brought by the state and Mr. Alvarez's pleas of not guilty. The preliminary hearing for case number RL46809 will be scheduled for March 9, at 9:00 am, in this courtroom." The judge then looked up, made a passing glance to both tables, and said, "Any issues with that, gentlemen?"

Both Chris Matula and Darrin Tressel said in unison, "No, your honor."

"With regards to bail, Mr. Alvarez, given the nature of these charges, I will set bail at five hundred thousand dollars."

Hector wasn't sure if he was supposed to answer or react, but since he knew that bail didn't matter, in his circumstances, he simply stood and stared forward.

"Your honor, given the severity of the charges and the defendant's previous record, the state would ask you to consider denying bail," Chris Matula said, looking at the table in front of him, rather than at the judge.

"Your suggestion is noted, but my decision is final. Bail set at five hundred thousand dollars. I'll expect preliminary briefs from both of you no later than four days before our preliminary hearing date. Other than that, I think we're all set."

"Thank you, your honor," Matula said in a voice that sounded like he was disappointed with the decision on bail.

"Thank you, your honor," mirrored Tressel.

"Next up, Judy," Judge Henderson said to the midget in front of his desk, requesting that she call the next case for arraignment.

"That's it?" Hector said to his lawyer, as the bailiff came his way to return him to the wooden bench.

"Yes," Tressel answered. "I'll be in touch soon so we can talk about the prelim."

With that, Hector was led by the arm back to spot behind the wooden wall, and watched as Darrin Tressel left the courtroom behind Chris Matula.

Once both lawyers stepped outside the massive courtroom doors, Darrin Tressel yelled forward to Matula.

"Mr. Matula, this guy doesn't want a plea," he said, causing Matula to stop immediately and turn around. "He wants a full, long trial, and he couldn't care less about his actual sentence."

"Are you kidding me?" Matula said, breaking into a beaming smile. "That's perfect, actually."

"How do ya figure?" Tressel said, somewhat surprised by the assistant DA's comment.

"'Cause I wasn't planning on offering him one, anyway." Matula reached out and tapped Tressel on the arm and said, "Alvarez fucked up, literally, and it's my job to see that he never bothers another citizen in this state, ever again."

Tressel knew he was right, but he never guessed the DA's office would take the time to push this case to trial. As Matula disappeared down the marble stairs, Tressel felt his stomach tighten to a knot. A humiliating public trial, which would certainly not end well for his client, was certainly not the way to further Darrin Tressel's legal career.

Wednesday, 9:40 am -- Interstate 10 Westbound, California

Frank could feel the little bastard vibrating on his leg. He knew better than to leave that stupid phone in his pants when he was driving, as the seat belt always put up a fair fight, ensuring that most calls ended up in voice mail. As he wrestled with the belt, and the fact that his front pants pocket allowed his phone to slide all the way down to the side of his leg, he secretly vowed to buy a car with Bluetooth, in the next month or two.

Fortunately for Frank, this time the seat belt lost, and he was able to answer the call.

"Yeah," Frank barked, now mad at the caller for causing his freeway battle with cellular technology.

"Uncle Frank?" Bobby's voice was uncharacteristically quiet and unsure.

"Yeah, Bobby, it's me," Frank responded. "Sorry about the short temper, but I couldn't find the damn cell phone," Frank admitted. "I guess all the kids are right; it's time for this old man to get Bluetooth."

"Where are you?" Bobby asked, ignoring Frank's comments about his temper and the need for wireless help.

Frank immediately found it strange that Bobby had asked about his location, because Bobby's whole life was focused on knowing the exact location of almost every member of the family.

"Ten west," Frank explained, "just left Santa Monica and headin' for Pasadena to meet someone for lunch. Where are you?"

"Mission Hospital," Bobby said somberly.

"Everything okay, Bobby? You sound like you're in a church or something."

"Frank, it's Papa," Bobby said.

Just the fact that Bobby was speaking so quietly, and so slowly, was enough to alarm his uncle, but now that Bobby had called him "Frank," it was clear that there was a problem.

"Bobby, what's up? Don't play games; what's going on?" Frank said anxiously, breaking with his usual slow, steady cadence.

"Papa passed over this morning, Frank."

"Holy shit, Bobby," Frank said instantaneously. He knew this day would come, and he had told himself to be strong when it did. He knew Papa's kids would need a strong, steady figure when Papa passed away. Unfortunately, when he got the news from Bobby, he forgot everything he'd planned and simply reacted.

Frank took a quick look over his shoulder and crossed two lanes of highway traffic to reach the median on the side of Interstate 10. His hands were already shaking, and he knew he had to get out of traffic. Since Bobby had not responded to Frank's short outburst about the news, he tried to compose himself and try again.

"Bobby, when did he go?"

"About thirty minutes ago," Bobby said, with no elaboration.

"Was he," Frank asked as delicately as he could, "at peace when he passed over?"

"I think so," Bobby said. "He slid into a coma about an hour ago, and the doctors said he was comfortable but declining."

"Did you get a hold of the family on time?" Frank asked, almost wishing he hadn't as soon as it left his mouth. Bobby already put too much pressure on himself to be the perfect son, and handling his father's death perfectly was an unrealistic objective for any son.

144

"I was waiting to get some more information about the coma before calling everyone, but unfortunately, he passed real quick."

"Nothing you can do about that, Bobby," Frank answered, trying to make sure that Bobby didn't carry any more burden. "How can I help?"

"Nothing to do right now, Uncle Frank," Bobby said quietly. "I've called the funeral home, and I'm going to meet with them tomorrow morning. Once I do that, and get a better understanding of all the things we'll have to do, I'll give you a call."

"Bobby, did you get the chance to speak to Papa this morning," Frank asked curiously, "before he went downhill?"

"Yeah, I did," Bobby replied and then stayed silent for a few seconds.

Frank stayed quiet on the other end, as he had learned to do with Papa. He knew there was more to come, but that Bobby would continue speaking only when he was ready.

After some uncomfortable silence, Bobby finished his thought. "Papa wanted you and I to be sure we gathered the full family for the Alvarez prelim. He said he did not want Ang going to the proceedings and to make it clear to the DA that she should not be a witness." As Bobby spoke, his voice gained both pace and volume. "Papa said not to fail him on this. He said to get the boys to the prelim and make it obvious to Alvarez that he messed with the whole family, not just Angelina."

Frank could hear the passion and persistence in Bobby's voice as he recounted the final conversation with Papa.

"Bobby, you leave that up to me, okay," Frank said in a clear statement, rather than a question. "You focus on Papa's funeral and helping the family manage the transition, and I'll focus on the Alvarez thing."

When Bobby didn't respond to Frank's proposition, Frank added the final touch.

"Bobby, trust me, I will not let Papa, or you, down on this thing. Alvarez will have no doubt what he's dealing with at the prelim."

DAY 28

Thursday, 2:50 pm -- Los Angeles County Superior Court

Despite the nagging pain in both knees, Judge Henderson walked up the one flight of stairs and down the long hallway to the office of his basketball buddy and peer, Judge Herbert Singleton. They rarely made a physical appearance at each other's offices, and in fact, other than stopping by to pick him up for weekly hoops game, Henderson couldn't think of a single time he'd made a personal call on his buddy. Phones were just too convenient, and fifteen individual stairs provided enough separation, given the state of his ligament-free knees.

After a slight knock, Henderson entered the office door, which led to Singleton's senior clerk, Pam Duggan.

"He in, Pam?" Henderson asked as he limped into the waiting area.

"He sure is, Judge Henderson," Pam said with a surprised, nervous look on her face. "Did you guys have an appointment that I forgot to book?"

"No, just stopping by for a quick chat."

"I think he's on the phone," Pam lied, "so let me just check; a quick second." Pam put up one finger, as she slid back from her desk and headed to Judge Singleton's door. Henderson smiled, thinking how all clerks were alike -- spontaneous meetings or calls threw their whole day for a loop, as they preferred to have their judge's calendars laid out to the minute.

Pam disappeared into Singleton's chambers for no more than thirty seconds, then reappeared, giving Judge Henderson a wave.

"Come on back, Judge Henderson," Pam said with a big smile. "He said as long as you were not here to collect on previous bets, he'll see you."

"He can't afford all the bets he's lost to me," Henderson said as he moved slowly to the door. "Thanks, Pam."

"Hendo, you get off the elevator on the wrong floor, or do you need some of my Aleve?" Judge Singleton chuckled as he stood from his desk and circled around to meet his friend.

"No, I've got the equivalent of a Tylenol IV drip down in my chambers, so I think I'm good there," Henderson responded with a smirk.

"So what's up, my friend?" Singleton asked as he waved Henderson over to the two oversized chairs that faced each other.

"Remember the Alvarez thing we talked about at the Y a week or so ago?" Henderson started. "You know the kid that tried to rape a girl at Oyster a while back?"

"Nice memory, Hendo," replied Singleton. "I told you about the case, remember?"

"Yeah, yeah, I remember. It turns out the assistant DA, Half-Pipe, is all fired up to try the case, no matter what," Henderson said, looking for some reaction from his peer. "It's a slam-dunk case, as far as I can tell, and I don't think some court-appointed rookie is going to pull a rabbit out of his hat."

"So what's your point?" Singleton said, trying to guess the answer to his own question. "You've got to sit through weeks of testimony and evidence in order to get to the same outcome the two parties should agree on right now?"

Henderson knew his friend would understand, but he was surprised how quickly he caught on. "Exactly -- a fantastic waste of taxpayer money, judicial time, and use of jurors," responded Henderson, a little animated as the simple thought made him agitated. "Have you had any luck getting the DA to plea, or a defendant to accept a plea, when both sides are dead set against it?"

"Your only option is the one you already know about," Singleton said flatly.

"Meaning make it real clear that the evidence makes this a slam dunk, and trying the case is a waste of time?" Henderson asked, wondering if he was following his peer.

"Yep, that and making it real clear that not agreeing on a plea would make returning to your court for future cases an unpleasant experience for the two attorneys," Singleton replied with a slight smile.

When Henderson looked to the ground to internalize what Singleton had said, Judge Singleton added, "Hendo, sometimes lawyers get locked on the case at hand, but you can help them understand that not addressing this case appropriately may just piss you off in future court appearances."

"Got it," Henderson said, standing slowly to signal he wouldn't take any more of his buddy's time.

"We've talked about his before," Singleton said as he walked his friend to the door. "These regulars are a pain in society's ass. We keep sending them away for short stints, but they keep coming back. Until they give us enough ammo to put them away for life, we'll just keep playing this little game of in-and-out."

DAY 28

<u>Thursday, 10:15 am -- LA County Jail</u>

Hector had just awoken from a midmorning nap when he heard the familiar yell from the guard as he walked down the corridor. Soon Hector was being led to the same set of conference rooms where he'd first met Darrin Tressel. As the guard escorted Hector into the conference room, Tressel was waiting, with a fresh yellow legal pad in front of him.

"Hello, Hector," Tressel said as his client slid into the chair across from him.

"Long time, no see," Hector said sarcastically. "Oh, I'm sorry -- long time, no see, your honor," he laughed.

"Very funny, Hector," Tressel said with a smile. "Since we don't have much time between now and then, I want to explain the prelim process to you."

Hector looked about as interested as the guards, but Tressel knew that Hector needed to understand the process. With the pen he had laid on a new legal pad, Tressel began doodling diagrams as he spoke.

"A preliminary hearing has one primary objective," Tressel began, as he wrote the number 1 on his legal pad, "to determine if there is enough evidence to send the case to trial."

Hector gave his attorney a lazy nod, and Tressel continued.

"The district attorney needs to prove that they have enough evidence to charge you for assault, kidnapping, and attempted rape." Tressel paused for a second to catch his breath, and to make sure his client was still paying attention. "If the judge feels there is adequate evidence, he'll set a trial date and reconfirm bail at that time."

Tressel tore off the first page because he'd scribbled all over it. Hector smiled because Tressel really hadn't written anything that mattered; he just seemed to be more comfortable scribbling while he spoke.

"The prosecutor can call witnesses, enter physical evidence, or anything he wants -- just like he'll do at an actual trial. Our job is to refute that evidence and cross-examine his witnesses to show is evidence is weak or flawed in some way. That make sense?" Tressel said, looking up from his legal pad to his client.

"Yeah, but if I actually want a trial, do I still care about this prelim shit?" Hector asked, completely serious.

"Hector, you are not pleading guilty to these crimes, right?" Tressel shot back, staring at his client.

"You told me not to," Hector replied, a bit confused.

"Listen, when we get to trial, if I don't try to defend you, this thing will be over in a day or two, and you'll be gone for a very long time. Do you understand this?" Tressel said, trying to shake some sort of reason into his client.

"I get it," Hector answered, "but I want a trial, so why would I fight at this prelim thing? Wouldn't I save my fight for the actual trial?"

Tressel sat back and put both hands behind his head. This was the craziest damn case he'd ever seen. Hector certainly did understand the process, and beyond any shred of normalcy, he couldn't care less about the outcome. In law school, they never cover handling the client who is clearly guilty, who doesn't want to defend himself, but who won't accept a plea.

The truth was, if Hector wanted a trial and would only defend himself in order to produce a longer trial, the idea of not pushing back at the prelim actually made perfect sense.

"Hector, I don't know what to do with you," Tressel admitted openly. "You don't want to defend yourself, but you do want a long trial, where the prosecution will most certainly overwhelm a jury with evidence against you."

"That's right," Hector said without any emotion, "that's what I want."

Tressel rubbed his face with his hands in disbelief.

"I have that right, don't I, Mr. Lawyer?" Hector asked earnestly.

Tressel wasn't sure how to answer that other than with the truth. "Yes, Hector, you do have that right."

Friday, 2:50 pm -- Los Angeles County Superior Court

Helen stuck her head inside Judge Henderson's chambers while lightly knocking on the door. She waited for him to finish whatever paragraph he was reading, and look up from his desk. Years of practice had taught her not to talk while he was reading, as he had an uncanny ability to block out all distractions while reading legal briefs. As she had warned most of his visitors, "You can scream, sing, or shoot a cannon, but if he's reading, he's not hearing you."

When Judge Henderson removed his glasses and looked up at her with a slight smile, she began.

"Larry, Curly, and Moe have all arrived for your three o'clock meeting," she said with a smile.

"Give me about two minutes to finish up here, and then bring them in," he requested.

"You got it," Helen said in her normal perky way. "Need any more caffeine?"

"Yes, please," he said excitedly.

"What form -- coffee, tea, Diet Coke?"

"Diet Dr. Pepper," he said, "but put it in a coffee mug before you bring it in. It will look more dignified."

"One dignified Dr. Pepper coming up," she said, giggling as she slid back out and closed his door.

Henderson organized the papers on his desk into neat piles and then stepped around his desk to welcome his guests. As he reached the door, Helen was once again knocking and reentering with his guests behind her.

"Judge Henderson," Helen said loud enough for all the participants to hear, "District Attorney Robbins, Assistant District Attorney Matula, and Mr. Tressel are here, per your request."

Helen stepped aside and let them enter. Each stopped to shake Judge Henderson's hand and exchange greetings as they entered.

"Gentlemen, grab a seat there at the couches," Henderson said, pointing to his seating area with two couches, two chairs, and a large round coffee table. "Did Helen offer you something to drink?"

"Yes, we're all good," Geoff Robbins said, speaking for all three of them.

The judge waited for all three to be seated before he took his usual spot in the oversized chair that faced the coffee table, with a sofa on either side. The lawyers were neatly dressed in white dress shirts and differing shades of red ties. Only DA Robbins wore a suit jacket as well, with a red handkerchief protruding from his breast pocket.

Judge Henderson had called the meeting, so he began. "Gentlemen, I appreciate you taking the time to meet here today. Usually I apologize for downtown traffic, but I'm assuming each of you could simply walk here from your office, huh?"

All three nodded yes and maintained their eye contact with the judge.

"Next week, we commence with the preliminary hearing for Mr. Hector Alvarez, so I thought I'd take this opportunity to set some clear ground rules and expectations," Henderson continued.

Matula and Tressel nodded and glanced at each other, as if this was a standard comment from a judge. DA Robbins, who realized this meeting was anything but ordinary, was the first to respond.

"Judge Henderson," Robbins started, "when you say expectations and ground rules, what specifically do you mean?"

Chris Matula had been frustrated and embarrassed when his boss had informed him that he would be joining the meeting. Matula was afraid that Robbins' presence would imply that the DA was not confident that he could handle the meeting on his own. What's more, he knew that Tressel would come alone -- which he did.

But now, only two minutes into the conversation, he was glad that Robbins was there. He had the experience and the confidence to ask any question and challenge Judge Henderson on specific legal points, if necessary. Matula knew that Robbins and Henderson had some sort of personal relationship from their years of working for the state of California, but with Judge Henderson you could never tell if familiarity was a positive or a negative.

"I'm glad you asked that, Mr. Robbins," Henderson replied, obviously keeping his responses with Robbins formal for the sake of this meeting. "Specifically, I want to share what I expect at this prelim and the ground rules I expect both attorneys to respect." Even though Robbins had asked the question, Judge Henderson was clearly directing his response to Matula and Tressel.

"Let's start with prelim ground rules," Henderson said, sounding very conversational and informal. "I have read the briefs, and it's clear that there is critical evidence, and first-hand witness discovery, that will drive this case."

Both attorneys assumed he was talking about the physical evidence from the park -- Hector's weapons, Angelina's body marks, and her missing phone. Since Officer Patrick was the only witness other than the defendant and the victim, they knew the judge's reference was about him.

"Mr. Matula, this is not a trial, and I assure you, I will not allow you to try to turn it into one," Judge Henderson said with a fatherly stare to the assistant DA.

"Your honor, I ..." Matula began to respond, but was immediately interrupted by the judge's hand and his much louder voice.

"Please, Mr. Matula, let me finish my entire point, and then I will give you ample time to respond." As the judge lowered his hand, he adjusted his seat and appeared to be trying to remember where he'd left off.

Chris knew he'd hear about his anxious response. Robbins was always telling him to time his responses better, and make sure others have completed their thoughts, so that they are mentally ready to hear a rebuttal.

"The objective here is to determine if there is adequate evidence to bring these charges, and that such evidence is not nullified by facts from opposing counsel. I expect no more than one witness by each side, and no more physical evidence than was present on the night in question." The judge stopped to make sure both sides had fully understood his point before continuing. "I certainly realize that character witnesses, friends, and family may be part of your trial strategy, but it will not be part of your prelim strategy."

After checking both the facial reactions and body language of his audience, the judge said, "Are we perfectly clear on that?"

Again it was DA Robbins who asked the question they were all thinking. "Your honor, your directions are quite clear, but I'm not sure I follow your intentions," he said gingerly, hoping not to upset the man who would soon be listening to this case. "If we feel there is much more evidence, and rationale, to bring these charges against Mr. Alvarez, why would we want to limit the discovery of those elements at this time?"

"Mr. Robbins, this particular case involves a defendant that was arrested with weapons in hand, after using a Taser gun, and binding the victim to a piece of playground equipment. If the physical evidence and testimony of any, or all, of the three people present at the park playground cannot move this case to trial," he said, making it very clear that his guidance on this topic was not open for discussion, "then all the character witnesses and all the circumstantial evidence in the world won't change it."

Before any one of the three could respond to what he'd said thus far, Judge Henderson turned his attention directly to Darrin Tressel.

"By the same token, Mr. Tressel, if you cannot adequately refute the physical evidence and the testimony of the arresting officer, or perhaps the victim herself, don't waste our time with alternative theories and family members."

Judge Henderson sat back and let each side digest his points. He could sense that both Tressel and Matula were confused and a bit upset, but neither was willing to challenge the judge, given his position.

"So to be clear, your honor," DA Robbins said, to break the silence, "you want each side to limit its witness list for the prelim to no more than one witness each?" Robbins clearly emphasized the word one in such a way to communicate his disbelief and frustration on this point.

When Judge Henderson did not respond immediately, Robbins finalized his question by adding, "And regarding physical evidence -- you're saying we limit the prelim to only what was found at the park, or on the victim or defendant?"

Tressel had to admit that he was relieved DA Robbins had come. Not only was he not used to a personal meeting with a superior court judge, he didn't want to leave confused by his directions.

"I'll say it again," the judge responded sternly, "as plainly as I can." Again he turned his shoulders toward both Tressel and Matula, "the only witnesses needed at the prelim are the individuals that were present at the scene -- no more. The only evidence needed at the prelim is the evidence from the crime scene."

He sat back, looked at Robbins, and finished with, "I believe that should be crystal clear, to both parties."

Robbins nodded yes, while the other two attorneys avoided eye contact. As irregular as the request was, Robbins had to agree with the Judge Henderson's synopsis -- it really was as simple as Officer Patrick and the crime scene evidence. Anything more than that was just grandstanding at this stage in the process.

"Now, let's talk about my expectations for the two of you," Henderson said, clearly moving on to his next point, while vaguely waving at Tressel and Matula.

"I fully expect both of you to work diligently," he said and paused for effect, "yes, I said diligently, to find a reasonable plea bargain."

Both lawyers had noticeably anxious expressions as Judge Henderson paused and glanced around the table.

"I think we all know that a long, drawn-out court case would likely not be a valuable use of the state of California's money, and your time. If, Mr. Tressel, your client is fully aware of the case against him, I should think a lawyer of your caliber will have no trouble helping him to understand the benefits of a quality plea."

Both Matula and Tressel looked as if they wanted to say something, but neither did.

"Mr. Matula, I'm sure you and Mr. Robbins can get a substantial sentence in this case and free the DA's office for more challenging dilemmas than this."

Judge Henderson now sat back and clapped his hands together one time. He had said what he wanted to say and was comfortable that his message was understood.

"So, gentlemen," the judge said, wrapping things up, "can I assume we've had a clear meeting of the minds here today?"

Matula knew he should simply stay quiet and let Tressel be the first to speak. He knew Robbins was silently telling him to stay quiet with the stern glare he was giving him. But no matter how much he knew better, he couldn't hold back.

"Mr. Tressel has already informed me that his client will not accept a plea, regardless of the charge, or time served."

All eyes turned to Tressel, who felt trickles of sweat forming around his collar and under his arms. He was surprised that Matula had turned the tables on him, but he couldn't blame him for the approach. The real truth was that he was sorry he hadn't thought of it first.

"That is true, your honor," Tressel admitted without any emotional connection to the content. "My client has informed me that he wants a long trial, and will not accept a plea before that trial ends."

As the judge digested that comment, Tressel added, "Although I should mention that Mr. Matula informed me that no plea was going to be offered anyway."

Judge Henderson rubbed his hands together as if he was trying to keep them warm. It was clear he was upset, but he was obviously trying to think through his reaction before responding.

"Okay, fellas," he began, clearly trying to keep his emotions in check as he spoke, "you two are talented attorneys, but you are also both very young." Henderson was looking down at the table as he spoke. "You will likely be in my courtroom many times in the years ahead, and I'll expect three things from you, if you're going to have a successful career with me."

He gave both lawyers a threatening stare as he continued. "Are you ready?" he said, making both lawyers quietly wonder if they should be writing this down.

"Number one, always respect the legal process in my court," he said, and waited for their visual confirmation.

"Number two, always respect the witnesses and jurors in my courtroom." Judge Henderson now put up three fingers and paused until both attorneys were fully focused on him.

"Number three, always respect the effort and money of the state of California when deciding which cases will require my time."

Henderson looked at Robbins, but couldn't tell if the DA was engaged in his statements or lost in his own thoughts.

"You two are talented attorneys, and I have no doubt that if you commit to finding common ground on this case, you'll not only find it, but you will also be able to convince your side to accept it."

Tressel and Matula glanced at each other without a word. Judge Henderson's message and his threat was quite clear -- don't waste my time with cases that don't need a trial. Get past your hang-ups on this, and bring me a plea before you waste California taxpayer money, or a judge's time. Do this, or deal with an angry judge for years to come.

It sounded simple, but both attorneys knew it was more complicated than Judge Henderson wanted to hear.

DAY 32

Monday, 8:05 am -- Los Angeles County Superior Courthouse

Frank saw Bobby walking up the street toward the courthouse. As usual, Bobby was moving with the grace and the pace of an Olympic athlete. As he'd been instructed, Bobby was nattily dressed in a black double-breasted suit, with white shirt and glossy red tie. His thick black hair, dark black sunglasses, and black suit cut an impressive image against the bright blue sky.

Frank knew he could count on Bobby being early -- and he was right. Bobby started up the courthouse steps at 8:05 am, even though Frank had asked him to arrive at 8:30. It was for that exact reason that Frank had the entire male Constanzio clan arrive at 7:45 am at the front doors of the Los Angeles County Courthouse.

Frank knew that the doors of to any municipal building would not open until 9:00 am, but he wanted to leave no doubt that the Constanzio family would be first in line and able to secure the first few rows in the courtroom.

Bobby reached the top step and broke into a huge smile, as he removed his sunglasses. The sight stopped him in his tracks, and he looked as if it almost brought him to tears. Bobby looked down at his feet for a few seconds, trying to compose himself, and then looked to Frank.

"Baa-beee," Frank said, stepping forward to hug his oldest nephew, "how did I know you'd be early?"

Bobby was still speechless as he grabbed Frank and hugged him with all his strength. Frank started to release the oldest Constanzio boy but realized that Bobby wasn't letting go. Frank knew the extra-long embrace was a combination of thank you and sorrow over the passing of Papa. Because Bobby needed some time to compose himself, Frank

161

kept hugging and whispered in Bobby's ear, "I love you, Bobby, and I'm here for you, just like I was for Papa."

"You did good, Uncle Frank," Bobby whispered back. "This is exactly what Papa wanted."

Bobby finally released his uncle and took a step back. Staring back at Bobby were twenty-seven male Constanzio family members, ranging in age from fifteen to eighty-one years old, each dressed in a black double-breasted suit with white shirt and red tie. Each stood tall and proud, and together they created a powerful, unified force.

"Papa is proud this morning," Bobby announced in a booming voice, "because his family comes together to stand as one."

Bobby slowly scanned the crowd of family members, stopping to make eye contact with each. He wanted every one of them to feel his gratitude and the importance of this morning, and he knew he could accomplish that with the right connecting look.

"I lost the bet." Bobby's younger brother Dante laughed, breaking the silence of the full group. "I said you'd be here forty-five minutes early, but Frank said thirty minutes."

While the full family chuckled, Bobby grinned and added to their laughter with his response. "I got here over an hour ago, but I went for coffee at the bagel shop down the street."

With everyone laughing over Bobby's anal predictability, each began to hug the oldest Constanzio boy, one at a time. While an occasional court employee would pass them and enter the police-guarded front doors, the Constanzio family members were the only visitors, at that point, waiting the for 9:00 am opening.

Frank had already provided the group his three, very specific instructions for how they would handle the morning. One, they needed to be the first twenty-five to thirty people at the front doors. Two, nothing questionable was to be brought into the courthouse, as they used a metal detector at the entrance and Frank wanted to make sure the authorities had no reason to slow their entrance. Finally, number three, each Constanzio member was to walk straight to the courtroom when the doors opened, with no diversions to the restrooms or to make phone calls. Frank made it clear that the first few rows of Judge Henderson's courtroom needed to be filled with family.

After seating, they were to remain completely quiet for the entire proceeding, but to never take their eyes off Hector Alvarez. Papa was clear that Hector Alvarez should understand that he had messed with much more than just Angelina -- he had messed with the entire Constanzio family. Frank had understood Papa's point, and he was sure that the family would make quite a visual statement, and if they stayed quiet, Judge Henderson would have no reason to address them in the audience.

After Bobby had hugged every member, and said his share of personal "thank yous," he returned to Frank's side and waited patiently for the courthouse to open.

"That little fuck better pray he goes straight to prison," Bobby muttered so that only Frank could hear. "And for a long, long time."

DAY 32

<u>Monday, 8:47 am -- LA County Jail</u>

This morning had been like no other thus far, at the LA County Courthouse Jail, for Hector Alvarez. Early in the morning, one of the guards had arrived with two different sets of clothes and a couple of exciting questions -- did Hector want a shave, and did he want a shower?

Hector knew that today his preliminary hearing would begin, but he expected to be in the same orange jumpsuit with the same two-week stink. While his hands were cuffed in front of him, Hector enjoyed a shave, compliments of a police guard who administered shaving cream and shaved his face with a disposable Bic razor. The shave was soon followed by a long, hot shower that even included shampoo. He had to admit that simply cleaning his body put him in a much better mood. He knew that today would simply end by the judge assigning him a court date for his trial, but he felt better now that he looked like himself and he'd lost his fourteen days of body odor.

When he returned from the shower, he saw two different sets of clothes laid out on the bunk in his cell. Both were from Hector's apartment, and both had been worn very sparingly in the past. Hector quickly assumed that Darrin Tressel had gone to his apartment to pick out clothes for his hearing. Probably not knowing Hector's preference, he'd sent two choices. Hector smiled as he looked at the two sets of clothes -- both very dressy by his standards. Given these choices, his lawyer was obviously saying, "Please look your best." This might be like saying, "your honor," Hector thought to himself. He could actually hear Darrin Tressel's voice in his head saying, "It can't hurt to show the judge some respect."

On the left was Hector's one and only black suit. He'd only worn that suit three times in his life. His brother, Juan, had forced him to buy it when his second cousin had invited them both to her wedding in San Diego. After that, Hector had only worn the suit twice -- both times in the last month, and both times brought back painful memories. He'd worn it to meet with the guy to discuss Juan's funeral plans and pick out the wooden casket. The only other time was at Juan's funeral.

Hector folded up the suit, placed it on his pillow, and began dressing in the second option that Tressel had provided -- khaki tan Dockers, with a blue short-sleeve button-up shirt. Tressel had also provided Hector's all-black Air Jordan sneakers to go with either outfit. Hector chuckled to himself, guessing that Tressel had searched his belongings looking for dress shoes, only to find that Hector didn't have any. When Hector wanted to dress up, he either used his all-black Air Jordans or his black work boots. Knowing that he'd worn his work boots to Oyster Park that night, and that they were probably locked up in some evidence room, these were Tressel's only option.

About the time Hector was ready to put on his shirt, the police guard appeared, to uncuff his hands long enough to slip it on and button it up. Once dressed and recuffed, Hector was led across a long indoor bridge that crossed above First Avenue in downtown LA and connected the jail to the courthouse.

Hector was then placed in a holding room with one chair and two doors -- the door he had entered, and the one he assumed he'd exit. He couldn't hear a thing in the room, which made him believe it had been created for just that purpose.

After about a ten-minute wait, with just him and the police guard in the room, there was a loud knock on the door he had not entered. The guard opened the door and stepped to the side, letting the courtroom bailiff slide in. The bailiff was quite a bit older than the other guards Hector had experienced so far. He was forty-five or fifty years old, by Hector's guess, but he was as strong as any man, at any age. Despite the long brown sleeves, black tie, and button-down collar, there was no hiding the ripples of muscles in his arms, shoulders, and back.

"Alvarez, Hector?" the mountain of a man said sternly as he reached out to grab Hector's arm.

"Yes," Hector said, trying to sound tough and not intimidated.

"Shut your mouth; follow me; speak when spoken to." With that, the bailiff firmly led Hector out the door and into Judge Henderson's courtroom.

DAY 32

Monday, 9:10 am -- Los Angeles County Superior Court

Hector had been in a courtroom many times. In fact, he'd been in this exact courtroom just a week ago, but today was unmistakably different.

First, there were no other inmates being led into the courtroom -- just Hector. Both tables that faced the judge's stand were occupied. Darrin Tressel sat at one table, and three guys in dark suits were at the other.

As the bailiff led Hector to the middle of the court, and then turned right to head to Tressel's table, Hector was startled by what he saw. Almost every member of the audience looked the same. It was an alarming sight, and Hector felt himself actually gulp in some air when he saw it. Every member of the audience was male, dressed in a black suit, and Italian.

It took Hector a minute or two to figure out what he was looking at. And once he figured it out, the loneliness of life without Juan, his protector, was more prevalent than ever before. As Hector turned to sit at Tressel's table, he froze for a second and thought about making a gesture or yelling something to the Constanzio family, in memory of his lost brother.

After thinking it through, he turned around and sat down. He realized that no one cared what he had to say -- no one remembered what he could never forget.

DAY 32

Monday, 9:25 am -- Preliminary Hearing Begins

Hector was surprised how brief both attorneys were in their opening remarks. The short tree-trunk of an attorney who was representing the state of California had kept things pretty simple, and focused only on the chronological facts -- phone, park, Taser, cop, arrest. He had shown very little emotion and provided very few details. He simply outlined the timeline of that memorable Friday night.

The only time the prosecuting attorney even raised his voice was when he finished, saying, "The evidence is overwhelming to support a full trial of Mr. Alvarez, and that evidence will result in a quick and substantial decision on every charge."

As he listened, Hector quietly congratulated himself on how he had lured Angelina away from her friends. The stolen phone, the text messages, and even the fake green Lexus had been brilliant. That cop showing up, completely by mistake, was the only thing that wasn't perfect. Hector had turned around and scanned the audience a couple of times during the opening remarks, but he hadn't seen Angelina. Probably buried in the middle of the Italian black-suit brigade, he figured. He looked forward to staring into her eyes when he got the chance.

Tressel's comments had been even more brief than Matula's. He plainly stated that there was no evidence of any sexual contact from his client to the victim. He said that the lack of sexual contact could be confirmed by the arresting officer, the doctors at Mission Hospital, and the victim's statements. It appeared to Hector that Darrin Tressel wasn't going to put up much of a fight on the assault and kidnapping, but was clearly focused on nullifying any rape-related charge.

"Mr. Matula," the judge bellowed from his elevated perch well above the rest of the courtroom, "you may call your first witness."

"Thank you, your honor," said Chris Matula as he stood and placed both hands in his suit pants pockets. He looked down at his legal pad on the table and said, "The state calls Officer Dennis Patrick, of the Pico Rivera Police Department."

Hector craned his neck to get a good look at the cop, but he didn't see anything -- other than twenty to thirty sets of Italian eyes looking straight back at him. He turned back toward the judge and saw Officer Patrick was already standing next to the witness stand. "Where did he come from?" Hector whispered to his attorney, but Tressel neither looked at Hector, nor offered a response.

As Hector stared at Officer Patrick, he had to admit that nothing about him looked familiar. Granted, it had been late, and a night full of emotion, but Hector did not recognize the man. At maybe five feet ten inches tall and probably two hundred pounds Patrick wasn't nearly as big as Hector had remembered. While he couldn't remember the face, he could still feel the flying tackle that had flattened him, and separated him from his Taser gun. Hector had many nights in jail to rethink the Oyster Park struggle, and his best conclusion was that he should have used his Taser gun on the cop. The cop would have been out for long enough for Hector to get away, and the message to Angelina's family would clearly have been sent.

As Patrick raised his right hand and swore the oath, Hector was surprised that he'd let a cop that size manhandle him so easily.

"Officer Patrick, can you please state your name and occupation for the court record?" Matula began.

"Officer Dennis Patrick, of Pico Rivera PD," the officer answered confidently as he glanced up at the judge. "I've been a patrol officer in the town of Pico Rivera for approximately seven years."

"Officer Patrick, can you tell us why you were at Oyster Park on the night of February 12?"

"Sure," Patrick began in a relaxed, conversational tone. "I tend to visit three locations pretty regularly on Friday and Saturday nights, given the likelihood of teenager gatherings."

Before he could continue, Matula chimed in, "What three locations are you referring to, Officer Patrick?"

"I patrol the Village Walk Theatres, the outdoor mall, and Oyster Regional Park, sir," Patrick announced to the full audience. "Kids tend to congregate in these areas on the weekend, so I figure a little police presence is a good thing."

"As a parent, I not only agree, but I thank you," Matula said with a slight grin.

Officer Patrick simply smiled and gave a "your welcome" nod.

"When did you arrive at Oyster Regional Park on this particular Friday night, officer?" Matula continued.

"I believe it was just after 10 pm, sir," Patrick said, admitting he didn't know the exact time as he stretched the word believe in his response. "I tend to troll these areas with my window down a bit, so I am able to hear activity that I might not be able to see."

"Can you please describe for the court, in your own words, what you heard and what you saw at Oyster Regional Park that night, officer?"

"Okay," Patrick said as he sat upright in his chair, preparing himself for the full answer. "I heard some rustling noise in the playground area that is just to the right of the main parking lot. I slowed my squad car to a stop so that I could hear a little better." Officer Patrick took a quick breath, as if he had expected Matula to interrupt him, but when he didn't, Patrick continued.

"Then I heard a loud buzzing sound," he said, wrinkling up his face in a squint to suggest the sound confused him. "To be honest, it sounded sort of like a bug zapper. So I turned my window-mounted floodlight toward the playground to shed some light on the scene." Patrick was clearly proud of his story thus far, and he sat back and waited for the question he knew was coming.

"Officer Patrick, when you turned your floodlight to the playground area, what did you see?" Matula asked, right on cue.

"I saw a person bent over a small piece of play equipment and a man standing directly behind that person," Patrick said very slowly, choosing his words carefully. "The man was holding something in his right hand, and he had his pants pulled down below his knees."

"Officer Patrick, is the man that you saw in the park, standing behind the person bent over the playground equipment, in this courtroom today?" Matula asked as he stepped to the side to give Dennis Patrick a clear, unobstructed view of the defendant's table.

"Yes, he is," Officer Patrick said and then pointed directly at Hector. "He's right there."

Matula let that comment sink in for a second, and then continued. "So you saw the defendant, Mr. Hector Alvarez, behind the person who was bent over the playground toy, and his pants were pulled down. Were Mr. Alvarez's underpants also pulled down, officer?"

"Yes, he was naked from his waist to his knees, sir."

"What happened next?" Matula walked over to the stand, in front of the judge's bench, so Patrick's gaze would be closer to the intended audience, Judge Henderson.

"Well, I jumped out of my squad car and shouted for him to freeze," Patrick said, waving his hand in Hector's direction, "and then I ran up to assess the condition of the person bent over the little wall."

"What was that condition?" Matula interrupted.

"First, I found it was a young female with no clothes," he said, looking up at the judge as Matula had instructed him to do during their multiple briefing sessions. "She was bound to the playground apparatus by very thick plastic zip ties. She also had her wrists bound behind her back. It was obvious that she was unconscious at the time, but when

I felt her wrists, I did feel a strong pulse." Officer Patrick closed his eyes, as if he was seeing the entire scene in his head.

"Then what, Officer Patrick?" Matula encouraged Patrick to continue.

"I called it in for backup," he said, seemingly snapping back to the present and following Matula's direction. "I called for medical help and officer backup, and then I turned and pursued the male suspect."

"I thought you had requested that Mr. Alvarez freeze," Matula said for a little dramatic effect.

"I had yelled freeze, but the suspect had started to run away as I approached," Patrick said, noticeably picking up the pace as he clearly remembered the anxiety of the moment. "Luckily, he had tripped when he tried to run. He was having some trouble getting his pants up, and that slowed him down," Patrick said with a trace of laughter.

When Patrick realized that Matula was only staring at him and not planning to insert another question, he continued. "When I ran at him, I saw he was holding something black in his right hand. I wasn't sure if it was a gun, so as I got close, I simply tackled him," he said, turning to the judge, "quite hard, in an effort to dislodge the weapon."

"Were you able to dislodge the weapon?" Matula said in a voice that suggested he was on the edge of his seat with anticipation.

"Yes. It turns out it was a C2 Taser gun. At that point, I cuffed Mr. Alvarez and read him his rights."

Matula walked back to the prosecutor's table and was digging through a dark brown box -- the kind lawyers typically use to transfer files. Lifting a Taser gun from the box, Matula asked, "Officer Patrick, is this the Taser gun you found Mr. Alvarez carrying that night?"

Judge Henderson made his first interruption at that point. "Mr. Matula, I hope you don't plan on dragging out every piece of evidence at a pre-lim-in-ary hearing," he said, slowly emphasizing every syllable of the word, to reinforce the fact that this was only a preliminary hearing.

"Unless Mr. Tressel plans to cross-examine on the validity of each item, I'd suggest we simply move on."

"Your honor," Matula pleaded, sounding more like an adolescent who had been told he could not go out and play, "I plan to bring the actual playground structure into the courtroom so that Officer Patrick can show the exact position of the victim, defendant, and all the weapons in question."

Judge Henderson did not take time in his answer. It was swift, and it was quite definitive.

"Mr. Matula, I am quite capable of understanding that the victim was bound to a structure, with the defendant standing directly behind. I am aware of the weapons we've discussed so far today and the others you've addressed in your prelim briefs." The judge was clearly not done, but he took a second to catch his breath and to make sure both lawyers were still with him.

"Now, if Mr. Tressel questions the location, questions the binding of the victim, or questions the existence of weapons, I'll allow you to do whatever you feel is necessary in your closing."

The judge took a long, serious look at Darrin Tressel and continued, "So far, I haven't seen the defense question those aspects of the case. With that said, Mr. Matula," he concluded and shot a serious, threatening look to the prosecutor's table, "I'd strongly suggest that you move along. I don't intend to try this case today, but rather to simply review the facts."

Matula was clearly staggered -- not because the judge had questioned his case or the validity of his evidence, but because he was eliminating the dramatic approach, which included the use of the playground structure and mannequin, that Matula had practiced for three nights straight.

With red patches on his cheeks and neck, and his hands buried in his pockets, Matula retreated to his table with a simple, "Understood, your honor."

Chris Matula grabbed his legal pad and flipped a few pages, trying to decide what direction to take next.

"After you arrested Mr. Alvarez and returned to the victim, was there anything else you noticed, Officer Patrick?"

"Yes, she had writing on her back, with red lipstick," Patrick answered.

"Lipstick writing, officer?" Matula asked, as if he was hearing it for the first time.

"Yes, on her back written in lipstick were the words No Limits," Patrick said, without emotion.

"Any reason to believe that the message was written by the defendant, Mr. Alvarez?"

"Well," Patrick said, in a sarcastic tone as he looked directly at Hector, "we did find the exact lipstick container in Mr. Alvarez's sock."

"Thank you, Officer Patrick, you've been extremely helpful," Matula said as he returned to his table and took a seat. "Nothing further, your honor." Matula then looked up judge and added, "Unless, of course, location and/or weapons are challenged by the defense."

DAY 32
Monday, 11:25 am -- Los Angeles County Superior Court

Judge Henderson checked his watch, as he could hear his stomach grumbling for food. With all the introductory paperwork, the opening statements by both attorneys, and Matula's consistent attempts to dramatize Officer Patrick's testimony, most of the morning was gone. He never felt it was fair to break for lunch in the middle of a lawyer's questioning of a witness, as that tended to alter any momentum or ability to link the witness' answers from beginning to end.

Henderson cleared his throat loudly and looked at both attorney tables to make sure he had the attention of both the prosecution and the defendant.

"Seeing as it's 11:25, I think this is a good time to recess for lunch," he said without requesting feedback. "When we return from lunch, Mr. Tressel, you can begin your cross-examination."

"As you wish, your honor," Tressel said with a perfect poker face, camouflaging any reaction to the early lunch. Even Hector couldn't guess whether the early break had bothered his attorney or had been exactly what he'd hoped for.

"This court stands in recess until 1:15," Judge Henderson barked to the entire courtroom as he banged his gavel on the small wooden pad that sat on his desk.

At that point, the bailiff quickly crossed the courtroom to secure a grip on Hector, while Tressel loaded his numerous legal pads into his briefcase.

"See you in about two hours, Hector," Tressel said without looking at his client.

175

"Come with me," the muscular bailiff said as he pulled up on Hector's bicep, encouraging him to stand.

Hector was returned to the tiny holding room with doors on both sides. The room contained just one chair and one table, which reminded Hector of the chair-desk combo units that he'd experienced in school. On the undersized table was a green food tray that held a paper plate, plastic silverware, and an individual-sized carton of milk.

Hector realized that his lunch break was going to be spent eating a cheese sandwich, tomato soup, and milk in a room just large enough for him and the prison guard assigned to watch him.

"One fifteen," the bailiff said sternly to the guard posted inside the holding room. Hector saw the guard check his watch, and although he had no visible reaction, Hector assumed that the guard dreaded these two-hour stints in the tiny defendant room.

Judge Henderson had quickly escaped to his chambers via the well-concealed door behind his courtroom desk. As he removed his robe and hung it in the closet, he smiled as he spotted the items on his coffee table. Helen had brought a large Cobb salad and a Diet Coke -- his favorite lunchtime meal when taking a courtroom break.

"Eat your roughage, drink your caffeine, and catch up on your reading." Helen's voice surprised Henderson, who was caught in a quick daydream. She had entered his office with her hands full of legal briefs. His startled reaction must have been noticeable, as she smiled a big, toothy grin and said, "Hey Kobe, maybe you should go caffeine-free today."

"Helen, you read my mind," Judge Henderson replied with a return smile to his senior clerk. "My stomach has been grumbling for a Cobb salad all morning."

"Guaranteed to relieve knee pain and increase vertical leap," she said with a laugh.

"Impossible on both counts, I'm afraid," the judge said, shaking his head no. "Unless you bought that salad at the same place Barry Bonds has been shopping, I think it will only solve my hunger problems."

"Wouldn't want you to fail the YMCA's urinalysis, judge," she said, to prove she understood the judge's uncharacteristic baseball reference.

"Helen, has my daughter called today?" Henderson asked, changing the subject abruptly as he sat on the couch to begin his meal.

"You haven't talked to her yet?" Helen quickly shot back, sounding a little shocked by the time that had passed since she first passed the message about his daughter's call.

"Just voice mail and text message exchanges, unfortunately," he said with a mouthful of lettuce, eggs, and ham. "No actual voice interaction."

"Want me to get her on the phone right now?" Helen suggested, hugging the legal briefs tightly against her chest as if to say, "these can wait."

"No, she's in class from eleven until one every day," he said with his head buried in his salad. "Cultural geography," he said, looking at Helen for her reaction, "whatever that is."

"How's the prelim going?" Helen changed the subject, sensing that the judge was a little depressed about not being able to reach his daughter. "Is it going to be a long one?"

"Not if I can help it," he barked. "I've given both of them a one-witness maximum, so I think we'll be done by late afternoon."

Helen was surprised they could finish so soon, and as a result, her mind raced with things she'd need to finish before Judge Henderson returned to his office.

"Do you want me to provide you with three or four date options for the trial?" Helen offered. "I could take a look now, so you'll have them when you return to session."

Henderson was actually caught off guard by her question. From the very first time he'd read the prosecutor's brief and reviewed the court record on Hector Alvarez, he'd assumed this case would be a quick plea. He hadn't even considered, not for one realistic moment, the possibility of this case going to trial.

"I think I was pretty clear with both sides that a plea is the right answer," he said, more to himself than to Helen. However, even as the words left his mouth, he wasn't sure how they'd left that point in his meeting with Tressel, Matula, and Robbins. He thought he'd been quite firm, but as he sat on his couch with his senior clerk waiting for direction, he couldn't be sure.

"Yes, you're probably right," he finally said as he set his fork on the table and rubbed his eyes. "I guess you'd better give me some dates."

"Will do," Helen said as she set the stack of briefs on the coffee table next to his lunch.

"That little shit is going to waste every minute and every dollar of taxpayer money he can before he takes a long-term vacation in prison," Henderson said aloud, staring at his lunch. "Then he'll get out and do it all again."

"Excuse me, sir?" Helen questioned, wondering if his previous statement was directed at her or was just the judge blowing off some steam.

"Oh, nothing," he said, taking a deep breath to ward off the exhaustion of the topic.

"You should see the first few rows of my courtroom," he said to Helen, waiting for her to ask him about more about it.

"Why do you say that?" she asked curiously.

"Let's just say Hector will get better treatment in prison than he'd get at home." The judge then opened the first green folder on the stack she had placed in front of him and reached in his breast pocket for his glasses.

Helen was a bit confused by his comments, but she knew that once he started reading, their conversation was officially over.

DAY 32

<u>Monday, 1:15 pm -- Los Angeles County Superior Court</u>

At exactly 1:15 by the clock in the tiny waiting room, a knock came from the door that entered into the courtroom. Right on schedule, the bailiff entered, nodded at the guard, and reached for Hector's arm. As Hector reentered, it was as if no one had even left. Each suit-bearing Constanzio family member was in the exact same chair he had been.

Like this morning, every set of eyes followed Hector as he was led to the middle of the courtroom and then to the defendant's table. Tressel had redecorated his table with yellow legal pads, in the same formation he had established in the morning. When the judge entered, causing the entire room to rise, it felt like déjà vu from just four hours earlier.

Judge Henderson banged his gavel firmly, and brought everyone back to their point of recess via a quick verbal recap. Then he appeared to reorganize the paperwork on his elevated desk and was ready to begin.

"Please bring Officer Patrick back to the witness stand," the judge said to no one in particular.

As Officer Patrick took the same seat he had occupied most of the morning, the judge gave him some final advice. "Let me remind you, Officer Patrick, that you are still under oath. Please answer each question loudly so our court reporter can capture your responses correctly."

Officer Patrick nodded his confirmation and adjusted his position, as if to get fully comfortable for a long cross-examination.

"Mr. Tressel, I assume you are ready to cross-examine the witness?" Henderson said to Hector's lawyer.

179

"I am, your honor."

"Very well," the judge said, waving his hand toward Tressel, "your witness."

Darrin Tressel didn't stand; he didn't sit up; he didn't even look up. He flipped a few pages on the legal pad directly in front of him as if he was nonchalantly looking for some missing information.

"Officer Patrick," he said, still looking at his own notes, "I just have four questions for you."

This bold statement caused Matula to lean toward his associates and mumble something that only they could hear.

Judge Henderson had seen this tactic too many times to get excited about an early exit. He hoped that Tressel's four questions didn't contain the eight or nine follow-up questions that usually trailed a bold statement like that.

Tressel's silence that followed his statement must have bothered Dennis Patrick a little, as he broke the silence, saying "Yes, sir, I'd be happy to answer them."

"One," Tressel began, now looking at the witness but not leaving his chair, "did you see Mr. Alvarez use the gun that you found him holding?"

The question caught Patrick a bit off guard, and his mind raced back to that vivid Friday night.

"No, sir," he said flatly, "I did hear a buzz, and ..."

"Thank you, Officer Patrick," Tressel interrupted loudly, clearly communicating to Patrick that no further explanation was needed, nor requested.

"Two," Tressel said, and paused for effect. "Did you see Mr. Alvarez bind, tie, or contain the victim, Ms. Angelina Constanzio?"

The use of Angelina's full name caused some noticeable chatter in the audience, which was likely disapproval from the male Constanzio clan, but not enough to require the judge to request courtroom silence.

Officer Patrick leaned his head back, as if to be in deep thought, "I saw her tied to ..."

"Officer Patrick," Tressel again interrupted, this time sounding more perturbed. "Yes, I saw Mr. Alvarez bind her. No, I did not see him bind her. It's just that simple, officer."

"No, I did not see him bind her," Patrick shot back loudly, emphasizing the see him part of his answer.

Tressel flipped to another page on his legal brief, and then leaned back in his chair and regained eye contact with the witness. "Number three, officer," he said, sounding as if he was gaining some personal confidence in the process, "did you see Mr. Alvarez touch Ms. Constanzio in any way?" Tressel punched the word any for extra effect.

"No, I did not," Patrick retorted, with a look that suggested that the officer would be happy to "touch" Darrin Tressel, when his questioning was over.

"Four, and finally, officer," Tressel said, while still sitting comfortably, "To our personal knowledge, has anyone suggested that Ms. Constanzio was touched sexually during the events that took place in Oyster Regional Park? Doctors, the victim -- anyone?"

"No," said Patrick, just before he was interrupted by Chris Matula.

"I object, your honor," Matula said, jumping to his feet. "Counsel is asking the witness for hearsay comments."

Tressel responded immediately, before the judge could react, "To the contrary, your honor, I assumed the officer was likely present at the hospital and during Ms. Constanzio's statement, so I was simply curious what he'd heard."

Judge Henderson raised his hand to the universal stop sign, to stop any further banter between the lawyers.

"Objection sustained. If you want to know what the doctors or the victim thought, Mr. Tressel, you'd simply read their statements, like the rest of us did," Judge Henderson said sternly to Tressel. "Now, Mr. Tressel, having reached your fourth and final question, can I assume you're done with this witness?"

Henderson figured Tressel had started this with his bold statement, so now he'd try to end it, based on that same statement.

"I am indeed, your honor, thank you. It appears to be quite clear that Mr. Alvarez had no sexual contact with victim, and other than to write a message on her back and scare her with his tactics, there is no reason to believe that a rape, or an intended rape, was taking place," Tressel replied, apparently confident with his cross-examination.

Judge Henderson was noticeably surprised, as he was certain that Tressel's four questions would lead to a full afternoon of follow-ups.

"In that case," Henderson stalled, as he flipped through some papers on his desk, "Officer Patrick, thank you for your time today. You are excused, sir."

After Officer Patrick left the stand and walked to a seat in the back of the courtroom, Judge Henderson said, "Mr. Tressel, you are free to call your witness."

"Your honor," Tressel said, coming to a standing position for the first time since the judge entered the courtroom after lunch, "the defense rests, as we are comfortable standing behind the lack of any eyewitness evidence to confirm any of the charges brought against Mr. Alvarez."

Tressel remained standing, awaiting a response or direction from Judge Henderson. Matula and his colleagues were busy whispering back and forth, clearly unsure how to react to Tressel's limited defense.

Judge Henderson turned and looked at the prosecutor's table. "Mr. Matula, are you comfortable concluding at this point, given the detailed briefs that have been submitted by both sides and read by me? In addition to the testimony heard today?"

Every fiber in Chris Matula's body said to push back, and call more witnesses, despite Henderson's chamberside chat. He knew he could overwhelm Tressel in evidence, but the guidance of his boss, Geoff Robbins, just kept echoing in his head -- "You don't win at the prelim, so don't try your case there. Share enough to secure a trial, but save your gunpowder for the trial. Don't let the defendant get a preview of your best stuff."

With Robbins' voice leading him, Matula stood up, placed his hands deep into his pants pockets, and looked to the judge.

"The state of California is comfortable that the briefs and the eyewitness accounts are sufficient to secure a trial on all charges, your honor." He then looked to his associates sitting at his prosecutor's table, to see if any wanted to get his attention. They did not.

"The state rests as well, your honor."

DAY 32
Monday, 2:05 pm -- Los Angeles County Superior Court

Judge Henderson took a quick look at his watch and saw it was only 2:05 pm. They'd only been back in session for fifty minutes. He was glad that his little chambers chat regarding a quick prelim had sunk in with the attorneys.

Unfortunately, he was also keenly aware that neither side had as much as offered a first volley as it related to a plea bargain. Both were dug in, and both were clearly set on a long, slow trail -- even though both sides agreed that Hector would eventually be found guilty on every charge brought against him. Judge Henderson looked out over his courtroom in a slow, steady scan, taking in all the sights.

Chris Matula, a young, competent attorney, full of passion and drive. He would drag out every possible character witness for Angelina and every aspect of Hector's attempted rape -- even though no one would question the innocence of the victim or the intentions of the defendant.

Darrin Tressel, a rookie lawyer in a tough spot -- a guilty client simply exercising his right to a full trial to delay his departure to a state penitentiary.

Multiple rows of Constanzio family members -- perhaps not perfect members of society, but they certainly had created jobs, businesses, and a sense of family in the Los Angeles area. No jail sentence could regain the personal comfort and free spirit that a seventeen-year-old girl had lost forever.

His bailiff, who for years had quietly struggled with the reality of "judicial justice." Both he and Judge Henderson knew that Hector Alvarez would be back in this courtroom again. He'd be ten years older and ten years tougher, and he'd be charged with crimes even more serious when he returned. The bailiff knew what every judge knew -- sometimes judicial justice took too long, and at a cost of too many innocent victims.

Judge Henderson ended his courtroom stare and his uneasy silence by opening his docket, which contained his calendar for the upcoming months. Helen, as instructed, had highlighted three different options for the Alvarez trial, and Judge Henderson circled one of the weeks.

"No need for a recess," he said loudly. "I am completely convinced that there is adequate evidence to support a jury trial on each of the charges brought by the state against Mr. Hector Alvarez."

Neither Hector nor his lawyer had any noticeable reaction to Judge Henderson's synopsis, and both continued to stare, emotionless, back at the judge.

"Grab your calendars, gentlemen," Henderson said to both Matula and Tressel. "We will schedule the trial to begin with jury selection on April 5 at 10:00 am."

The judge gave the attorneys time to rummage through their briefcases and locate their business calendars, but he really hadn't asked for their opinion on the dates. "Assuming there are no significant, conflicting issues," he said, while pausing to let the word significant hang in air, "we will begin trial on April 7."

Neither lawyer had a response, either to confirm or question the date, despite the judge providing adequate silence following his comments.

"That takes us to bail, and we'll be set to adjourn," Henderson said, beginning to wrap up. He looked up as if calculating, or taking the time to fully think through his next step.

"Mr. Tressel," Judge Henderson startled the defense attorney with a directed statement. "Do you plan to make a motion regarding bail and to request a release of Mr. Alvarez on his own recognizance?"

Hector looked at his attorney, who actually looked more confused than he was. Tressel put his hand on Hector's arm, as if to say, "Don't react just yet." After a few confused seconds, Tressel seemed to catch on to Henderson's line of questioning and rushed his answer, as if the judge might come to his senses at any minute.

"Yes, your honor, the defense moves to reassess Mr. Alvarez's bail and requests releasing him on his own recognizance."

Chris Matula shot up and literally screamed toward Judge Henderson's bench, "Your honor!"

"Yes, Mr. Matula?" Henderson looked irritated as he responded to Half-Pipe's interruption.

"Your Honor, Mr. Alvarez has been charged with multiple heinous crimes, and up until this point, he has been retained with a five-hundred-thousand-dollar bail. I don't understand the question that you posed to Mr. Tressel, and I object vehemently to any proposal to reduce the current bail position," Matula said, struggling to keep his composure.

"Your comments are understood, Mr. Matula, but that is why I have scheduled a quick trial. This way, the case against Mr. Alvarez can be tried quite soon."

Then, without waiting for Matula's rebuttal, Judge Henderson returned his gaze to Hector and Tressel. The courtroom was now buzzing from every corner. Matula was openly conversing with his colleagues, Tressel was clearly trying to get through to his client, and three full rows of Constanzios were whispering about the judge's comments.

Judge Henderson snapped everyone back to silence with three loud, piercing raps of his gavel.

"Silence," he bellowed, noticeably perturbed by the sudden courtroom outburst. "I will clear this entire courtroom unless we return to silence and," he paused, "stay that way until this court is adjourned."

The chatter stopped almost immediately, but Judge Henderson maintained a broad stare, as if looking to find one person bold enough to challenge his warning.

"Now," he said, returning to a normal decibel and trying to mentally return to where he'd left off. "Mr. Matula raises a fair point, and as such, Mr. Tressel, I will accept your motion, but only with the addition of home confinement."

Tressel could sense that Hector was about to shoot back with a smart-ass comment. He grabbed Hector's shoulder firmly to ensure he had his client's complete attention. Whispering in a voice that only his client could hear, Tressel said, "He's going to let you go until your trial date. Don't say anything stupid, Hector, just say 'Yes, your honor' when he asks if you understand. Say nothing more than that. Do you understand me?"

"Mr. Alvarez, I want to be very clear with you here today," the judge said, as he peered over his bench, with his eyes fixed directly on Hector. "Your trial will begin with jury selection on April 5, at 10:00 am. You will be required to report to this courtroom on that day, at that time. If you are not in this courtroom at 10:00 am on April 5, you will be arrested immediately, and you will face additional charges. Is that perfectly clear?"

Hector's mind was immediately racing, as he was completely confused by the entire process, but he followed his lawyer's guidance. "Yes, your honor."

"In addition, you will be constricted to home confinement while awaiting this trial, which means that you are not allowed to leave your home premises unless to flea a natural disaster -- meaning fire, earthquake, etcetera. Should you leave your home, you will be arrested and face additional charges, and will be placed in jail without bail." Once again the judge stared directly at Hector. "Is that abundantly clear, Mr. Alvarez?"

"Yes, your honor," Hector said aloud, while actually looking at his lawyer.

"Your honor, I am simply at a loss for words," Matula said in a near scream that matched the bright redness in his checks.

"Your objection was clearly noted and understood by this court," Judge Henderson said in a voice that suggested that this debate was now over. "Now, Mr. Matula, please return to your seat, and we will complete today's proceedings!"

After a short, uncomfortable silence, followed only by the sound of Matula's chair as he slid back to his table, the judge continued.

"Mr. Alvarez, should you be required to change your home residence between now and the April 5 court date, you'll need to immediately notify the court. Is that understood?" The judge waited for a response, but when he didn't get one, he added, "I'm sure Mr. Tressel can help you with that, should you have the need to relocate in the short period of time between now and then."

"Yes, your honor," Tressel quickly replied, to preempt his client from saying something that they both might regret. "Mr. Alvarez and I will certainly respect all the requirements of home confinement."

"Very well," Henderson said, sitting straight up in his chair and looking out to the entire courtroom. His face was noticeably whiter than it had looked all day, and he appeared to be a bit shaken. "The court will grant you OR, or release on your own recognizance, but only under the restriction of home confinement. You will be required to report to this exact courtroom on April 5 at 10:00 am."

The mumbling throughout the courtroom was noticeably rising again, as Constanzio family members were openly discussing the judge's decision. Henderson had his gavel in hand but had yet to use it. He sat looking over the court, and then directly at Hector Alvarez.

"This court is now adjourned," he said in a noticeably softer voice as he banged the gavel one final time and exited through his private door behind the bench.

The bailiff came toward Hector and produced a key that would presumably unlock his handcuffs. "You'll still need to follow me, so we can process your release papers," he said with a slight grin.

DAYS 32 - 39

FINAL SENTENCING

DAY 32

<u>Monday, 5:55 pm -- Santa Monica, California</u>

Chris Matula navigated his Honda CRV through the underground parking area in his condominium complex. Since his court session on the Alvarez case had ended much sooner than he anticipated, he decided not to go back to the office. The truth was Chris' head was spinning from the completely unanticipated events of the day. Based on Judge Henderson's one-witness mandate and Darrin Tressel's no-plea positioning, he knew that wasn't just a typical preliminary hearing.

Matula had spent days of preparation and over ten thousand dollars in cost to have the tic-tac-toe structure removed from Oyster Park so that he could use it in court. He wanted everyone to see the brutality of Hector's actions and the vulnerability of the victim, based on how she was tied to the apparatus. Matula was floored with Judge Henderson instructed him to "move on" and provide no further detail on the specific actions, weapons, or positioning of the individuals in Oyster Park that night.

If those had been the only significant rulings by Judge Henderson during the prelim, Matula would still have been frustrated, but at least he would have understood the judge's perspective. Henderson's final ruling, to eliminate bail and let Hector go until the trial, simply left Matula dumbfounded. How could a criminal with multiple arrests on his record, who was caught virtually in the act of a violent crime, be allowed to walk out of that courtroom today?

Matula knew that he needed to clear his head, and so when court was adjourned, he had driven straight to his favorite L·A Fitness gym for a long workout and an even longer shower, in the hopes of regaining some clarity. Unfortunately, as he pulled into his condo parking space and turned off the ignition, he felt as confused and betrayed as he had the minute he left the courtroom.

His reflections of the day were interrupted by the loud ring of his cell phone from his briefcase in the back seat. Looking down to check the caller's ID, Chris smiled and pushed "accept" to answer the call.

"If you're calling to get an explanation of today's events, Felix, I certainly can't help you," Matula said without a hello.

"Chris, it's Felix Bernard," said Detective Bernard, completely ignoring Matula's introductory response.

"Hey, detective," Matula replied, essentially agreeing to start the conversation over. "Were you in the courtroom?"

"Yep, I was there. Unfortunately, the Constanzio family reunion caused me to sit about five rows back," Bernard answered with a sarcastic laugh.

"Hope you wore your black suit and red tie, so you could fit in," Matula quipped.

"I can't afford the kind of suits they wear," bantered Bernard. "What was Judge Henderson thinking today? No bail -- what the fuck?"

Matula could actually feel relief when he heard Detective Bernard's reaction to the courtroom antics and the elimination of Alvarez's bail. He had started to wonder if he was too close to this thing, and maybe he was the only one who was having such a gut-wrenching reaction.

"I wish I knew, Felix," Matula responded exhaustingly. "I've been in a courtroom hundreds of times, but today was the most lost, and the most disappointed, I've ever been," he admitted.

"I just got off the phone with Robbins, and he suggested the three of us need to get a plan," Bernard challenged.

Matula had yet to call his boss, DA Geoff Robbins. He probably should have called as soon as court adjourned, but the truth was, he wasn't sure what to say. He knew Geoff would ask why Judge Henderson did what he did, and set Hector free -- but Matula had no answer for that.

"Shit, I haven't called him yet," Matula responded anxiously, obviously worried that Robbins got the news from someone other than himself.

"Yeah, I kind of figured that, by his reaction," Bernard said without apology. "I told him that you were probably as confused and frustrated as the rest of us. But you should give him a call."

"What did he say when you told him?" Matula inquired, to better gauge the reaction he was likely to encounter when he called his boss.

"I didn't wait for his full reaction. I told him he'd better decide if he wanted to prosecute Hector Alvarez, or simply send flowers." Bernard's comments caught Matula off guard, as he was waiting to hear more about Robbins' reaction to the news.

"What are you talking about?"

"Chris, if your defendant goes home tonight, you won't need to worry about trial documents and witness lists," Bernard said and paused to let Matula follow his direction. "He'll be dead well before any jury selection starts."

"What makes you so sure about that, Felix? It would be pretty risky to touch him now -- with all the focus that would bring," Matula said.

"Do you think the three rows of penguins in that courtroom today was some sort of welcome wagon? Alvarez screwed with the Constanzio pride and joy, their little girl. I wouldn't expect them to sit and wait for a well-worded plea bargain."

"What did Robbins think?" Matula asked, wondering if Geoff was as convinced as Felix appeared to be.

"He said that you and I should work closely with LAPD and Darrin Tressel to get Hector some added security, starting tonight. In fact, I think his actual words were, 'I guess we'd better keep that little shit alive; otherwise, we'll be knee-deep into a Constanzio investigation.'"

"Got it," Matula said, snapping back into the moment and mentally shifting into executional go mode. "Let me make some calls right now and get Alvarez some protection."

"Hey, Chris," Bernard said, prompting a reaction.

"Yeah?"

"Better make the first call to your boss."

Monday, 6:10 pm -- Grand Bridge Apartments

Hector couldn't believe he was about to walk into his apartment. When he woke up this morning, his only decisions were shower and shave. Now, twelve hours later, he was returning to his apartment, and he was essentially a free man.

Tressel had explained that he'd need to stay in his apartment and report to court on the date and time the judge had given; otherwise, he'd be locked up immediately, and more charges would be added to his case. Tressel offered his personal services to purchase any food and/or living supplies that Hector might need during his confinement.

Hector had thought about his apartment and the comfort of his bed many times over the past couple of weeks, but he'd already surrendered the thought of ever lying on it again. Tressel had been kind enough to drive Hector home and had stressed the importance of Hector taking all precautions to protect himself. There was no doubt that Angelina's family would like to see Hector pay, physically, for his actions.

As Hector walked up the two flights of stairs to his apartment, he withdrew the plastic baggie that the guards had given him when he left the jail. In it were Hector's personal belongings from the night he was arrested -- minus any evidence for the case.

The baggie contained only three things -- his uncharged cell phone, a pack of unopened Big Red gum, and the single key to his Grand Bridge apartment. Hector withdrew the key and hurriedly unlatched the door. While in jail, he'd told himself that he'd never see his apartment again, but now he was actually giddy with excitement to come home.

As he opened the door and stepped inside his apartment, his first visual was of his patio sliding door across the room. He saw Angelina's name written in lipstick, and in less than a full second, it all came rushing back to him -- Juan, Angelina, Oyster Park.

He turned to close the door behind him, but as he did, he heard a loud thud that sounded like the noise a baseball bat would make hitting a softball. The alarming noise started outside his head, but quickly traveled to a loud clatter that reverberated inside his brain. He tried to remain conscious as his legs went limp and would no longer support his body weight. Through a growing dizziness, he could see the floor rapidly approaching his face, but he simply couldn't make his arms reach out to cushion his fall.

In less than a second, the sound left his head -- along with his consciousness.

DAY 32

<u>Monday, 8:38 pm -- Thousand Oaks, California</u>

"Honey, it's Judge Singleton on the phone. Are you available to talk?"

Judge Henderson could hear the gingerly approach, and the worry in his wife's carefully selected words. First, her husband's unexpected early arrival home, and now his refusal to leave the basement -- let alone come to dinner. She could certainly see that her husband was hurting and seriously troubled, but he had yet to share his thoughts with her. She knew he'd confide in her when he was ready.

It wasn't the first time that the courtroom had rendered her husband helpless, but this was the first time he seemed so fragile, and so unwilling to begin his recovery.

"Honey, did you hear me? Judge Singleton -- do you want to talk?" she repeated as she stepped down to the bottom stair of the basement with her hand over the mouthpiece of the cordless phone.

"I'll call him back," Henderson said, without turning to look at his wife or breaking his stare at the blank television -- which hadn't even been turned on since his arrival earlier in the day.

DAY 36
<u>Friday, 10:45 am -- Pico Rivera Police Department</u>

Officer Dennis Patrick wasn't used to being so far out of his territory. For the past seven years, D-Pat (as he was known to his coworkers and friends) had been assigned to a twelve-mile radius in Pico Rivera, California. At one time, Pico Rivera had been considered a suburb of Los Angeles, but now that all these smaller cities had been swallowed up by the ever-expanding boundaries of Los Angeles, it was no different from any other LA district. In the case of Pico, it was 80 percent Hispanic, relatively poor (meaning most inhabitants had jobs that paid by the hour), and extremely tough.

Dennis would rarely let down his guard while on patrol in Pico, because the anti-police sentiment among certain Pico residents was high, and self-restraint was low. He had learned early on to pick his battles wisely in this area. If he wanted to, he could simply sit at specific street corners, parking lots, or alleys and wait for a drug transaction or domestic disturbance to come to him, but arresting fifteen-year-olds all day did very little to keep Pico safe.

Dennis proudly boasted that despite seven years on the job in Pico Rivera, he had only pulled his gun from its holster two times, and had only been forced to physically overpower a suspect once.

He'd witnessed things he'd never forget and forgotten things most people would never witness. He was proud of his record in Pico, and was even prouder of the relationships he had formed with some of the neighborhood's long-standing residents. Despite the poverty, racial tensions, and influence of gang-related activity, Dennis remained convinced that the overwhelming majority of Pico residents were good people, and they respected the job he did.

197

Like any city, or any assignment he might receive, he spent 90 percent of his time with the 10 percent of people who don't respect police, don't respect others, and aren't afraid to physically force their ideas on those who stand in their way.

Today, however, was the first time he'd been asked to leave his territory during an official shift. Sure, he had to be downtown LA to appear in court every few days or so, to represent the state on tickets or fines he had written -- or to occasionally testify as to certain evidence or conversations that he had been privy to -- but today was much different.

"D-Pat, the captain wants to see you, pronto," his shift leader, Sergeant John Nelson, had said as Dennis entered the locker-room facility at the Pico Rivera Police Department.

"You sure you got the right guy?" Dennis asked, wondering why the heck Captain Sturgess would need to see him.

"Probably needs a ride to the airport or someone to check to see if his wife is cheating on him again," Sergeant Nelson joked, as he could see that Dennis was a bit rattled by the request.

"Shit, if he needed to know if his wife was cheating, that's easy," said Dennis, "I'll just tell him I've seen your car at his house every afternoon this week, Sarg."

Dennis chuckled and gave the sergeant a joking forearm to the chest as he exited the locker room.

"D-Pat, I got no time to do the captain's wife," Sergeant Nelson yelled back as Dennis was leaving, "since your girlfriend has got me completely worn out."

Dennis kept walking. He enjoyed a good locker-room ribbing as much as the next guy, but in seven years on this assignment, this was the first time Captain Sturgess had ever requested a one-on-one meeting with Dennis, and he certainly wasn't going to keep him waiting.

As he approached the captain's corner office, his heart started pounding so hard that he was actually afraid it might be noticeable through his uniform. Now he wished he had armored up --meaning put on his flak jacket -- prior to coming to see the captain, as the jacket would have eliminated any noticeable heartbeats and probably made him look a little more official.

The captain's door was always closed -- always. Dennis guessed Captain Sturgess hadn't seen the training video regarding the open-door policy of the LAPD.

Dennis tapped lightly on the door and waited for a response.

"D-Pat, is that you?" the captain yelled.

"Yes, captain."

"Get in here," Captain Sturgess said in the friendliest tone he could muster.

Captain Sturgess never looked up as Dennis entered. "D-Pat, you remember that kid you caught putting the wood to that hot teenager?" The captain had a unique way of making a violent attempted teenage rape sound like a children's game of hide-and-seek.

"Yes, captain. He is awaiting trial right now," Dennis said as he reflected back to the gruesome rape scene he'd encountered at Oyster Regional Park. "He's a dead man. There's no better evidence than catching the kid, literally, in the act."

"He's a dead man, all right," the captain responded while diligently searching for a specific phone message, in a stack of fifty or so messages spread randomly throughout his desk.

"Here's an address in the IE. They need you there this morning," Captain Sturgess ordered as he handed Dennis one of the phone messages from his desk.

In Southern California the IE stands for Inland Empire, and specifically, San Bernardino and Riverside counties. The IE is just east, or inland, from Los Angeles and Orange counties, and is generally associated with hotter temperatures, cheaper land, huge industrial warehouses, and nightmare traffic for those who wish to commute from there.

"I need you drive out there first thing this morning and ID a body." With that Captain Sturgess finally looked up and made eye contact with Dennis.

"ID a body? What body?" Dennis looked at the address and couldn't think of who he might know in Riverside County.

"That's what they want you to tell them -- whose body is it?" the captain said, smiling at his own weak attempt at a joke.

"Just take a little drive, D-Pat. Get a nice, long look at the body and tell them if you recognize it. Just that simple."

Dennis was already racking his brain when the captain ended their conversation the way only Captain Sturgess could. "Dennis, if you're waiting for a more formal invitation to leave, it ain't going to happen. Now suit up and get your ass to that location!"

'Nuff said. One thing Dennis was sure of, this was certainly not going to be just another average day on patrol in Pico Rivera.

DAY 36

Friday, 11:05 am -- Chino Industrial Park, Riverside County, California

The Riverside County Medical Examiner turned into the warehouse office complex and carefully navigated her van between six or seven police squad cars randomly located in the parking lot.

The call to her office had said probable murder, so she had appropriately braced herself for what she might encounter. Now, in her fifth year on the job, Natalie Fulson wasn't rattled by much. Gang shootings, automobile collisions, and teenage drug overdoses used to freeze her in her tracks; but five years later, she had hardened her senses and was now able to categorize every crime or accident scene as "just her job."

"Morning, Nat," Officer Tom Kiley, or TK to his close friends, was the first to greet her. TK was always friendly, but today he seemed especially cordial. When he saw her get out of her van, she noticed that he quickly crossed the parking lot to meet her.

"Whadda we got, TK?" Nat said, assuming Tom had been at the scene for quite a while.

"We got something," TK said with noticeable caution and apprehension in his voice, "that is beyond description."

"Nat," he said as he looked back over his shoulder toward the loading dock door that opened to one of the warehouses, "this is some nasty stuff."

Natalie had long ago learned not to question patrol cops about the details of the crime scene, as they almost always included their own thoughts and biases about what happened. So despite TK's open-ended comment about what was in the warehouse, she decided to remain quiet and simply go see for herself.

"Anybody pick up for this one?" Natalie asked. If there was one thing that Nat could count on, it was coffee at a crime scene. Usually the first cop on the scene would rope it off and call it in. The second cop was usually responsible for taking quotes from witnesses or interviewing people in the immediate area. The third cop was the key to a good crime scene, because as patrolmen liked to say, "three means tea." Probably a carryover saying that dates back to Britain, where tea was an all-day drink, but regardless of where the saying originated, it was certainly still a habit for Nat's local police force.

"Trust me on this one, Nat," said TK, "this one is better off on an empty stomach."

TK's comments caught Nat a bit off guard. She'd known Officer Tom Kiley for almost four years, and in all that time she couldn't think of another crime scene, or accident scene, that had noticeably bothered him. Maybe he had been affected by previous cases, but he surely never let her, or anyone else, know it.

"Okay, caffeine can wait. Take me to your stiff," Nat joked.

Even as she said it aloud, she was disappointed with herself. When Nat first joined the coroner's office, it used to drive her nuts that the detectives, cops, and paramedics were so casual about victims. Terms like stiffs, floaters, beanbags, and piñatas used to make her cringe. A deceased human being was still someone's dad, mom, brother, cousin, or friend. It took her a long time to get used to the lingo of the crime scene, but she always secretly vowed not to become "one of them."

Now she was using a term like stiff before she even got out of the parking lot. She silently scolded herself as she followed TK across the lot.

"This warehouse has been empty for about a year," TK explained as they walked toward a raised loading dock, typically used for loading and unloading semi-trailers. "It used to be an office supply outfit that would cater to small businesses in the area. You know, paper, ink cartridges, envelopes, that sort of stuff."

"Why'd they move out? It seems like that kind of stuff would thrive in a business park area like this?" Nat questioned. She was always a little fascinated by how building tenants seemed to be constantly turning over.

"Office Depot moved in about eighteen months ago and essentially terminated all these small local operations," TK said as he pointed in the general direction of the Office Depot Superstore that everyone knew about -- and Natalie was no exception. "Big bastards move in, and the little guy either joins up, if he can," TK paused as if just saying it aloud was bothering him even more, "or finds a new career."

"You sound pissed, TK. You a secret investor in an office supplies operation or something like that?" Nat chuckled.

"No, no, no," TK said as if her question had actually been serious. "I have a neighbor that was in the hardware business, and his forced early retirement was courtesy of the Home Depot." TK stared at Nat, waiting for some kind of response, and when he didn't get one, he added, "I guess it just touches a nerve with me."

Natalie followed TK up the four or five stairs that led to the dock platform, and from there they entered through the fire escape door, which had been opened for them.

It was immediately obvious that the warehouse was empty, other than rows and rows of metal racking. Natalie was struck with how quickly all daylight seems to vanish when you step inside a huge concrete box, with no windows, thirty-foot-high ceilings, and only one open bay door.

"Please tell me electricity is still turned on," Nat pleaded, "as my normal shoddy work gets even worse when it's done in the dark."

One of the other patrolmen who stood by the open bay door chimed in. "Yes ma'am, but the lights in here are on candescent bulbs, so they take about ten minutes to kick in."

"Please, save the term ma'am for someone much older and much higher in rank," Natalie corrected. "When did you throw the switch?" Nat asked, so she could work backward against his ten-minute estimate.

"They should pop on any minute," said the young, baby-faced officer, who seemed somewhat embarrassed by his ma'am comment.

As Natalie and TK stepped farther into the warehouse, she could see that the metal racking reached all the way from the floor, to just three or four feet from the ceiling. The racks were painted orange and were bolted to the floor.

"All the way back here," TK said, giving her a half-hearted wave toward the third aisle of racking.

The farther they got, the less Natalie could see, so she tried to time her walk to keep perfect pace with TK. She listened to his boots against the concrete floor and tried to match each stride -- that way she wouldn't lose him or run into him.

Just as she was completely focused on her steps, the overhead lights of the jumbo-sized warehouse sprang to life. In an instant, the sixty-thousand-square-foot warehouse, perhaps the size of a football field, was completely visible.

Natalie's first view was of TK. He was looking almost straight up, and the look on his face was terrifying. Sometimes in her business, watching the reaction of someone else could actually be worse than looking directly at the victim. Unfortunately, as she followed his gaze to the scene above them, Natalie realized that TK's reaction was the absolute least of her problems.

While the dizziness she immediately felt told her brain to look away, she was unable to break her gaze on this unbelievable sight.

DAY 36

<u>Friday, 11:45 pm -- Chino Industrial Park</u>

Dennis was surprised at just how beautiful the landscape was on his drive from Los Angeles to Riverside. When his boss' boss, Captain Sturgess of the Pico Rivera Police Department, gave him the order this morning, he hadn't expected to enjoy the drive.

As usual, the captain had been pretty short and direct in his command, "Here's an address in the IE. They need you there this morning."

For about ten months of the year, the Inland Empire is also known for its desert-like temperatures, rolling hills covered with dead brush, and high fire danger. When the rest of the nation turns to CNN to see the state of California "on fire," the IE is usually a focal point.

However, the secret that all Southern California residents knew, was that every January and February, this great land would be rejuvenated. It might be only a couple of inches, or sometimes torrential rains that brought flash floods, but these two months of actual moisture would cause the dried-out mountains and valleys to spring back to life. The truth was, and Dennis was witnessing it firsthand, that in the months of March and April, southern California was as beautiful as any place on earth.

"No wonder no one ever leaves California," Dennis said aloud as he came through the valley on Interstate 91, which led him from LA to Riverside. His laptop computer, which was mounted in the front middle seat of his squad car, was giving him turn-by-turn directions and verbally reminded him to exit on Magnolia Drive, en route to the Chino Hills address that his captain had given him.

As he pulled into the business park address, Dennis quickly realized that he wouldn't need to squint and look for specific addresses on each warehouse building. There were eight patrol cars, two unmarked cars (probably detective vehicles), and one medical examiner van parked just outside the third warehouse on his right. Yellow caution tape was tightly pulled across an open loading dock bay door, and three patrolmen were gathered at what looked like an employee entrance door, directly to the left of the loading dock.

Dennis pulled his car right up to the loading dock bay and parked, in an effort to minimize his steps to the entrance. Screw it, he thought to himself, I've never been the key witness to ID a victim, so why park in back like just another cop?

His LAPD squad car and Pico Rivera lettering on the door had clearly caught the attention of the lingering Riverside cops.

"You're pretty far from home, aren't you, Pico?" said the youngest of the three officers gathered by the open bay door. He was standing with one foot on the first stair to the employee entrance and one foot on the parking lot.

"Figured it was a nice day for a drive," Dennis responded, as if to say "I can be as sarcastic as the next guy."

"Can we help you, officer?" The voice came from someone just inside the open loading dock door, but then quickly emerged from the inner sanctum of the building and walked up to the border that had been created by the rungs of yellow tape.

"Yeah, I'm Officer Dennis Patrick, and I'm here to ID a body. Sounds like the vic may be the same guy I arrested a couple of weeks ago, that's awaiting a rape trial," Dennis explained.

"Got it. I'm Officer Tom Kiley," the man behind the yellow tape said as he motioned to Dennis to come up the stairs with a wave of the hand. "Come on up, and I'll take you to him."

"Thanks," Dennis replied as he worked his way through the three-cop human maze that existed on the different levels of the stairs.

"Hope you haven't eaten recently, Dennis," Officer Kiley said with no hint of sarcasm.

"I'm planning on hitting a little Mexican joint on the way home. No place like Riverside for authentic Mexican food," Dennis said with a smile.

"You got that right," Kiley responded as he led Dennis through the warehouse, which was completely empty warehouse, except for steel racking that extended to the ceiling and had created obvious aisles when the warehouse had been in use. "You guys got all the great Korean, Indian, and Japanese places. Our only claim to fame is wildfires and more Mexican restaurants than Starbucks."

As they walked about halfway down the third aisle of racking, TK gazed up at the now-stiffening, and completely naked body that was hanging directly above them. Ropes extended from the victim's neck, each tied to the highest rack on opposing sides. From a distance, it gave the impression that the body was floating above the middle of the aisle, but from closer inspection, it was simply tethered perfectly between the sides.

"We were just about to cut him down, but the detectives and ME wanted to analyze the scene before we let him fall," said Kiley.

"Holy shit," was the instantaneous response from Officer Dennis Patrick. As he continued to stare, his mind was working feverishly to piece together what he was actually looking at. "What's wrong with his mouth?"

"Somebody wrapped his mouth about forty times with electrical tape," Kiley explained, as Tom had had a lot more time to grasp the entire situation. "Same with his wrists and ankles. Why use handcuffs if you have a couple rolls of duct tape handy, huh, officer?"

Dennis tried to chuckle in response to Kiley's comments, but his throat felt like it was full of sand, and his mind was still racing.

"I'm no doctor," Dennis said hesitantly, "but isn't he missing a couple of vital body parts?"

"Yeah, you noticed that too, huh?" Kiley said, reinforcing that Dennis had just stated the incredibly obvious. "The boys and I have checked this entire warehouse. We checked the dumpsters out back and every trash bin for a half-mile radius, and no sign of his missing testicles."

"Damn, I'd frown too," Dennis said in response to the distinctive, red markings on the exterior of the duct tape that covered the victim's mouth and nose, which gave the impression that he was frowning.

"Well, is he your guy?" Kiley asked, immediately returning Dennis' brain to the original purpose for his visit.

"Can't tell with the duct tape covering most of his face, and the fact that the majority of his head is MIA." It didn't take a coroner to see that someone had shot the victim directly between the eyes, and the impact of the close-range shot had blown off a significant portion of the back of his head as the bullet exited.

"Well, you said your guy was up for rape, right?" Officer Kiley remembered. "I'd say if this is your guy, his raping abilities have been altered permanently, and he won't be needing that court date."

All Dennis could do was nod in agreement.

DAY 39

<u>Monday, 10:25 am -- Los Angeles County Superior Court</u>

Helen used the tape gun to secure the top of the box she had packed with the last of Judge Henderson's personal belongings. She had to keep her head down and stay focused on the task at hand to keep her tears from coming back.

Judge Henderson's chambers had always been such a perfect mix of professionalism and personality. He'd hung his law diploma right next to his framed tickets of the Lakers' "three-peat" NBA championships. He'd always have a law book and a basketball on his favorite easy chair. As she scanned the empty shelves and naked walls, she was reminded of just how sterile a judge's chambers can be without a judge's individual personality.

"Did you get it all?" Henderson said as he appeared at his door and looked at the six boxes she had lined up on his desk. She had to admit that he looked pretty relaxed, and at peace with himself, standing there in his faded jeans, Nike sweatshirt, and seriously worn Adidas high-top shoes.

"Let's just unpack it all and go back to work, judge," Helen said, pleading with her boss to reconsider.

"Helen, when have you ever known me to change a decision that I have made?" he said with a smile that they both knew was hiding a series of emotions.

"Well, not many," she admitted, "but this is the first decision you've made that really sucks."

Judge Henderson loved Helen's loyalty, and he cherished her friendship. He knew they'd grow apart over time, but he had committed to help her find another good job, and would also do his best not to be a stranger in her life.

"Oh, how I wish that were true," the judge painfully replied as he thought about the impact of his most recent failed decision.

Helen understood his answer and avoided further discussion, as she could see the pain in her boss' face.

"The state of California will get weaker the minute you leave this office. You know that's true, sir." Helen believed every word, and she knew that nearly every employee in the building agreed with her.

"It's time for someone else to make a difference," Henderson said, completely unwavering in his response. "It's time for a new face, a fresh perspective; someone that can see only the law and not the past."

With his final statement, Judge Henderson walked over to his favorite chair and grabbed the basketball that he'd dribbled, spun, or carried for over ten years in his chambers. Tossing the ball to Helen, he smiled and said, "The ball's in your court now. Handle it with care, my friend."

DAY 39

Monday, 1:55 pm -- Riverside County
Medical Examiner's Lab

Natalie Fulson adjusted the headlamp that was strapped around her forehead. She looked more like a coal miner in this headgear, than the Riverside County Medical Examiner, but she didn't care. When Natalie was working on a cadaver in her lap, she wanted perfect lighting everywhere she was looking.

As the head coroner for Riverside County, she had experienced all types of accidents and criminal victims, but this one was like none she had ever seen.

She spoke aloud as she worked, since her lab was wired to record everything she said. By recording her spoken words, Natalie didn't have to pause to take notes, nor did she have to worry about punctuation or spelling. She'd simply load the Word document on her computer after an autopsy and then format, spell-check, and print the final report.

As she made her first incision, which started at the victim's larynx and finished at his waist, she started her verbal dictation.

"Case number RL46809," she began.

"Victim is a nineteen-year-old Hispanic male; bruising and lacerations on both the hands and ankles; clear evidence of a physical struggle."

Natalie looked at the victim's face, and recorded the disturbing visual: "Victim has one-inch-thick layer of industrial-strength duct tape wrapped over his mouth and nose, with screwdriver-size puncture holes at the nostrils, likely to enable air passage."

"On the external side of the duct tape, over the victim's mouth, red lipstick has been used to create the visual appearance of a frown."

Natalie took a step back to make one more overall observation before she focused on the internal portion of this autopsy. As she looked at the victim's groin area, she continued,

"Victim has been completely castrated, with a less-than-precision instrument. Cut lines are very jagged and suggest a tearing of the skin and tendons, an effort to remove the scrotum in its entirety."

She tried to keep her words as professional and purely medical as she could, but the truth was, this young man not only had his testicles removed from his body, but the incisions were obviously amateurish, and clearly done by someone who had no concern about the pain this would cause. The fact was, any effort to remove someone's testicles would cause a threshold of pain sure to force the victim into a form of traumatic shock. However, to do it this way, tearing the scrotum from the body versus cutting it away, was certainly done to maximize the pain; or said another way, to maximize the message.

"Patrolmen and detectives at the crime scene were unable to locate the testicles, and other critical internal fluid matter that was likely to have been produced from this wound." Natalie was proud of herself thus far, as she thought her voice and perspective remained purely medical.

Earlier that morning, Natalie had dictated the specifics of the victim's actual cause of death -- a single gunshot that entered the body exactly between the victim's eyes and exited the back of his cranium, taking roughly one-third of his cranial matter with it. Due to the clearly distinguishable burn marks on the forehead and bridge of the nose, it was clear that the weapon used in the fatal shooting was placed firmly against the victim's face when fired.

Natalie had decided to break this autopsy into two sessions -- so this morning she did a complete review of the gunshot wound, enabling her to focus this afternoon on the other issues with this victim. In this particular case, calling the removal and eventual disappearance of his testicles an "other issue", was a difficult classification, to say the least.

As Natalie progressed, she exposed the internal organs and followed the same procedure she always did with an autopsy of this sort -- stomach, heart, lungs, in that order; followed by spleen, intestines, and anus.

"Internal organs are normal in appearance, with no visible signs of trauma," Natalie continued as she propped the stomach slightly higher than the other organs, to prepare for her first organ evaluation. She took her scalpel and made two perfectly placed incisions, to allow her to fold open the stomach lining and analyze both its contents and its relative health.

"Stomach lining is pink and healthy and appropriately sized relative to the victim's weight," Natalie said aloud to the recording device. "Victim appears to have eaten just prior to time of death, as large amounts of undigested food matter are still present."

With that, Natalie grabbed a football-sized stainless steel bowl with her left hand and a pair of small medical tongs in her right. She reached into the exposed stomach to retrieve the first food item and place it in the bowl. As she took the first item from the stomach and held it high into the light, she was so startled she nearly reached a state of shock herself.

Her discovery, and immediate physical response, caused her to drop the bowl with a loud clang and knock her headband light to the floor. Despite her emotional and physical spasm, she retained the tongs in her right hand, and the element they had recently retrieved.

Natalie quickly set the tongs on the sterilized metal desk next to the victim and peeled off her latex gloves. Reaching into the deep front pocket of her medical smock, she grabbed her cell phone, and quickly dialed a number.

Once the voice on the other end answered, Natalie skipped any greetings and went straight to the facts.

"I found the testicles you were looking for." Even as Natalie said the words aloud, she couldn't believe what she was seeing.

A wave of dizziness overcame her, and she was forced to find a quick seat. Finding someone's testicles in his own stomach was shocking enough, but she couldn't imagine the kind of pain and torture a person must have been experiencing in order to actually swallow his own sexual organs.

CPSIA information can be obtained
at www.ICGtesting.com
Printed in the USA
LVHW101350061121
702618LV00015B/922/J

9 781449 016500